MERE
SMOKE

jonathan call

author of Stealing Tesla

ebook ASIN: B08VH5WP1P

Paperback ASBN: 978-1-7355394-2-3

Cover design by: Kip Richmond

To Chris,
Proud of you man.

But a Samaritan, as he traveled, came where the man was; and when he saw him, he took pity on him.

Luke 10:33

1

New York City, June 1935

I OPENED THE SAFE before tripping over the corpse. Had I kicked the body first, I would've left the box alone. Especially after what I discovered inside it.

Sometimes doing a guy a favor can blow up in your face.

First things first. Let me get this out of the way.

I am a thief.

Judge me as you may, but that's my career path. I'm what society would call a product of the streets. That's not an excuse, just an explanation, but make no bones about it, I am a thief. A good one. I learned from the best, my Pops. The slickest boxman in five boroughs.

His name was Harry C. Flynn, and I was named after him. Technically, I'm a junior, but nobody calls me Junior—thank goodness. They don't even call me Harry—not that I mind the name—but from the cradle I've been called Buck. Buck Flynn. Don't ask me how that came about. No one bothered to tell me. But please don't call me Bucky. I hate that. Only one person in this world calls me Bucky, but that's because I have no say in the matter.

I'll tell you about him in a bit.

Mostly, it was just me and Pops in this world. My mom died when I was just learning to crawl. I don't remember her much, except from some creased sepia photographs that my Pops kept in his wallet. She'll always be blurry and water-stained to me.

Pops was—what the pulp magazines call—a gentleman thief, like Raffles, or that French character, Arsène Lupin. At least that's how I like to think of Pops. Others may have a different opinion. Sure, I understand the 'rose-colored glasses' thing and I can over-romanticize his reputation, but he was a great Pops with a heart of gold...for a thief. He had a host of friends, some of whom were shady, I'll give you that, but most were just down-to-earth folk trying to scratch out a living; sometimes honest, sometimes not.

Pops went to work one day and got shot dead.

Work, in this case, was cracking a safe in an upscale brownstone in Brooklyn. The story goes, it was his shoes that betrayed him. They were a brand new pair of black oxfords he'd bought at the Thom McAn's on Broadway that same day. Apparently, they squeaked on him.

The safe happened to be in the bedroom where the house-owner and his wife were sleeping. Being a light sleeper, the squeaking shoes startled the fellow awake. He grabbed a .38 snub-nose that he kept in his nightstand and put a hole smack in Pop's chest. The police and medical help were called to the scene, but Pops died on the spot. Tragic.

I can't blame the homeowner. He was just doing what comes naturally when finding your home being burgled. Pops would've done the same thing had he found someone trying to steal his own stash—could they ever find it.

Sadly, the whole affair left me an orphan of the streets at thirteen. I'm not complaining, just telling you how it is. That was seven years ago, and if it wasn't for a few of Pops' friends helping me out here and there, I don't know where I'd be.

Oh, in case you're wondering, I always wear crepe-soled shoes whenever I do night work. Lesson learned. Thanks, Pops.

Like tonight. I was wearing my crepes when I stumbled over the body. Surprisingly, I didn't get any blood on them. The killer, however, messed up his shoes some and that fact alone eventually worked in my favor.

However, I wasn't wearing the crepes earlier in the evening when I first met Gustave Nordstrom. I was wearing my brown and ivory two-tone wingtips. That's because I wasn't on a job at that point. I was out on the town.

I had spent the evening at *The Famous Door*, a jazz club down on W. 52nd Street—what we call 'Swing Street'. Bob Howard was the headliner. I had a corner table, where I sat alone nursing a beer all evening, listening to him tickle the ivories and sing a few of his new songs, as well as some standards. I didn't have a date, but that's okay. I don't need companionship while listening to jazz. The riffs and key changes are company enough—and truthfully, sometimes girls just want to talk right over them.

I play a little clarinet myself. Not good enough to accompany Bob Howard at *The Famous Door*, but good enough to jam with some friends of mine now and then. Pops gave me my first clarinet when I was ten. He even paid for seven or eight lessons. I took it from there. I now own a Selmer Radio Improved B Flat, the same instrument that Benny Goodman plays. But don't tell him that. We shouldn't be mentioned together in the same paragraph.

I left the club around midnight, stopping briefly to chat with Socks, the club's doorman. His actual name is Herman, but everyone calls him Socks, don't ask me why. I've never been curious enough to ask about it. He offered to hail a cab for me, but it was a warm June evening and I felt like walking.

That was the decision that got me into the mess.

2

——◦——

I WAS COMING UP to my street when I spotted the poor sap.

He sat on a bench under a street lamp, his head in his hands like life had kicked him in the ribs too many times. His legs straddled a battered cardboard suitcase. He wore an oatmeal herringbone newsy cap and, as I drew closer, I noticed a split in the seam of his jacket at the shoulder and his trousers were scuffed and torn at the knee.

"Hey, you okay fella?" I asked.

"Leave me alone," he muttered through his hands.

I hadn't seen his face yet, but I could tell he had yellow hair and appeared to be fairly young, about my age—nineteen or twenty. He was a big guy though, that much was clear, even hunched over as he was. He had shoulders like a tractor. His hands were huge and scraped up with some blood leaking from the scrapes—fresh blood. I also noticed blood spatters on his jacket sleeve and a slight smear on his pants leg.

Normally I avoid people spattered with blood, but for a big guy, he looked pretty pitiful. I took a seat next to him.

We sat quietly for several minutes, listening to the city making its normal noise. Finally, he glanced my way. He was a good-looking kid, with a firm chin and sharp blue eyes and a smooth, wholesome face that had recently been battered black and blue. His lip was split, too.

"You still here?" he asked, annoyed.

I shrugged. "It's a free bench, isn't it?"

He mumbled something indistinguishable and turned away.

"What's your story?" I asked. "Did you get into a fight or something?"

"Look," he snapped, "If you're looking for money, I ain't got none, okay? So beat it."

"Whoa, fella. Just trying to be friendly here." Beneath his forlorn state, he was smoldering with anger.

He grunted. "Yeah, right! No one in this town is friendly unless they got a reason for it."

"So what happened? You get mugged? Someone kill your dog? What?"

"It's this blasted town. I shoulda never come here."

"New York? It's the greatest city on earth."

He gave a snarl of disagreement.

———————❦———————

It took a while, but I finally got him on my side. He told me his name was Gustave Nordstrom—Gus for short. Said he was from out of town and hadn't eaten in three days. I tempted him up to my place with promises of bologna sandwiches, cheese, and bottled beer.

"I don't take charity," he snarled.

"Bologna's not charity…its lunch."

For a starving man, he sure had a firm grip on his principles.

He finally agreed.

I live on the fourth floor in a corner apartment overlooking the street. The building has an elevator, but I rarely use it. The contraption is a small wrought iron cage that holds about three people. It's old and creaky, with a hand lever that rarely obeys the orders it's given, causing the cage to stall in-between floors, or ignore floors completely, and it crawls so painstakingly slow you tend to be much older by the time you reach your destination. I was going to ignore it this time, but Gus looked so famished I didn't think he'd make the four-story walk. So I led him to the cage instead. The guy probably weighed over two hundred pounds, and I wasn't about to carry an oaf his size up those stairs.

Ten minutes later, we got there.

He sucked up four sandwiches pretty quick, along with an entire block of cheese. He passed on the beer, but I had a bottle of milk in the icebox, which he downed in a few gulps. I scraped up a bag of potato chips and a box of Ritz crackers and got them in front of his face before he tapered down—a hungry, feral beast can be dangerous.

After he was well fed, he went into my bathroom to scrub himself clean.

While he was in there, I heard a dull scrapping sound coming from behind me at the window on the alley side of my apartment—the window leading out to the fire-escape. I looked over and saw the tabby cat that always comes scrounging around for food. He's a pretty animal, with gray fur flecked with black, a pure white throat, and soft blue eyes. But let me be clear! I don't own the beast, yet he thinks he lives here. I got up and opened the window for him and he leaped in. He brushed up against my legs, mewing for a treat.

"You're too late," I said. "I don't have a drop of milk in the house. Someone beat you to it."

I sat down and he jumped up into my lap, anyway. And that's where he was when Gus came out of the bathroom. Gus looked better—his face was still battered, but clean. His lip had stopped bleeding.

"That's quite a collection," said Gus, peering into the living room. "Where did you get all that?"

He was looking at my lock and key collection. He meandered over to it, staring with admiration. It is quite a collection, if I must say so myself.

Across the wall of my apartment are several square shadow boxes filled with various types of padlocks and vintage lock sets. Most are antiques. I have over four hundred locks. They are categorized and arranged according to size, make and model, and artfully displayed behind glass. Some are combination locks, some are keyed locks.

Three separate frames are for skeleton keys, grouped at their finger-grips and elegantly fanned. One as tiny as a baby's finger, another as long as a grown man's arm. Don't ask me what kind of door that one locks. I don't have a clue, but I like to think it could be a dungeon of some sort.

There are also a few glassed-in frames containing thousands of keys arranged in swirling paisley patterns—key art, I call it. Some paint, some sculpt. I design and paste.

"Wow," said Gus. "Are you a locksmith or something?"

"Or something," I equivocated.

He came back into the kitchen, bringing his bruised face with him. The welts grew into a smile when he saw the cat.

"What's his name?" he asked.

"I don't know. He's not mine. But he shows up a lot, and I call him something different every day," I said.

"A new name every day?"

"Sure. Pick one."

"Puff," he offered.

"Puff?"

I thought it a bit sissy and unoriginal, but seeing how it would be the beast's name for only a day—and the day would be over in twelve minutes—I let it slide.

Gus sat back down at the kitchen table. His lap must have looked more appealing than mine, because 'Puff' instantly deserted me for him. I had opened a bottle of Knickerbocker beer for myself, so I offered him one as well.

Gus was gently stroking the cat. "I don't drink alcohol."

"Never?"

"Never. Do you have any pop?"

I frowned. We call it soda in my neighborhood, but I wasn't about to get into *that* argument. I found two bottles of 7Up in the cupboard. They were warm, and I couldn't account for how long they'd been hiding up there. But he took one anyway.

And then Gus told me his story.

3

———◆———

Gus, it seems, was a heavyweight prizefighter. He hailed from a small town outside of St. Cloud, Minnesota. Apparently, he'd punched the snot out of everyone in the mid-west and had never lost a fight. They had a nickname for him back home: Nordstrom, *The Storming Swede*.

A fight promoter from New York had passed through Chicago one night and caught a bout that Gus was having with some poor schlep from Cleveland. The other guy had been taller than Gus, had a longer reach, and outweighed him by forty pounds, but that didn't matter. Gus had him on the carpet in less than a minute. The promoter was impressed. Slipped Gus a card with his name on it. Told him to look him up in New York. Promised him buckets of money.

The stuff of dreams.

The promoter's name was Manny Greenstreet. I'd never heard of him, which is strange because a friend of mine is in the fight business, so I'm familiar—at least by name—with most of the movers and shakers in the boxing world around New York. My friend, Nick Terrano, is a former welterweight champion and now owns a gym down on W. 28th. He was also a friend of my Pops, and he let me sleep in the gym once in a while after Pops got killed.

So when a name gets mentioned that I've never heard before, my suspicions get itchy.

Gus, on the other hand, was excited about the prospects of having a New York promoter backing him. His family back home were farmers from way back. But farming had taken a dive when the depression got going and Gus's dad had to take work as a meat cutter just to keep the bank from taking the farm from under them. The winnings from Gus's fights helped, but the family thought that if Gus could make it big time in New York, their worries would be over.

Gus's folks—supportive Swedish parents that they are—scraped together all the money they had in the world, drove him to Minneapolis in their flatbed truck, where he climbed into a bus that took him to Chicago; from there, he rode a train into New York.

That was three days ago.

However, when he got here, he quickly learned that Manny Greenstreet was a sleaze bag liar (I know, you're shocked! Shocked to hear that such an animal exists in New York). Yes, Manny Greenstreet was a promoter, but not in the traditional sense. His sport wasn't boxing at all; it was wrestling. Professional wrestling, where fat-gutted men bounce each other off the canvas while wearing costumes meant for Halloween.

Of course, good old Manny didn't tell Gus that until after the kid had signed a contract, and after Manny had taken all of his cash as a 'down payment' for publicity. The contract was an exclusive that gave Manny Greenstreet all the rights to Gus's life and bodily fluids.

Realizing the truth left Gus dumbfounded. He hadn't signed up to be a wrestler and tried to relay those feelings to his new manager.

"I told him I didn't know a thing about wrestling," Gus told me. "He said he'd make me famous, and that *The Storming Swede* would be the biggest thing in wrestling. As big as some character named, *The Golden Greek*."

"Jim Landos," I said. "He's a famous pro-wrestler."

"Never heard of him. I just want to box. I don't know nothing about wrestling. Mr. Greenstreet told me..." (yes, this corn-fed kid from Minnesota was still being respectful towards the scumbag) "...Mr. Greenstreet told me I would have to wear a costume. He gave me a pair of leotards and an animal skin cape, and a headdress with a set of cow horns on it, like a

Viking hat. Then he handed me a pair of underpants that he wanted me to wear on the outside of the leotards. On the outside!"

"What did you do?"

"What could I do? He'd taken all of my money. I didn't have enough for a sandwich. I agreed to do one match on the condition that he would refund me my cash—minus expenses for the publicity for that one night. I just wanted to get on a bus for home."

And then Manny dropped a moral bombshell. He told Gus that he had to take a dive for his first match.

"He wanted me to hit the dirt for some idiot in a cowboy outfit," said Gus. "I don't take a dive for anyone. It's dishonest."

Greenstreet told him he would pay him an extra five dollars to take the dive, on top of the ten he was paying him for the one fight. Gus refused.

"I told him to just give me my money back and we would tear up the contract."

Yeah, like that was gonna work.

Greenstreet started screeching at him, yelling things like, "I own you, you dumb rube!" and "I've got a contract! I'll take you to court, you stupid rutabaga!"

That was it. Gus refused to wrestle at all and stormed out—just like a Storming Swede, I suppose. That was three days ago.

He spent three days and two nights on the street with no money, no friends, and too ashamed a call back home.

He came to the end of his rope tonight and went back to Manny's office to have it out with him. He wanted out of the contract and his money back, tonight! Manny Greenstreet laughed in his face. He took the contract out of his desk drawer, waved it under his nose, told him he was running the contract up to his lawyer first thing in the morning, and then locked it away in his office wall safe.

Gus was furious by this point and showed Greenstreet just how furious by overturning his desk and breaking a couple of legs off of it.

Manny Greenstreet, of course, lives in a world where this kind of thing happens pretty often, and as such, keeps a wall of muscle at his disposal. Scumbags don't last long in New York without having a crew, and his crew happened to be professional wrestlers. It took five guys to do it, but they finally threw Gus out on his ear, and they gave him a good pummeling in the process.

And that's when I came into the picture.

By the time Gus had finished with his story, we had moved into the living room. He was sitting on my sofa, next to my lock and key art collection, and I was across from him in my armchair with my feet up on the coffee table. I had only taken two sips of my beer, but there was a reason for that.

It was nearly two in the morning and I could see that Gus was all in. His head was bobbing, and he could barely string cohesive sentences together. I grabbed a blanket from the bedroom and told him to sleep on the sofa. He didn't argue and was out like a lamp in seconds. He didn't even take off his shoes and jacket.

The reason I passed on the beer was that I had heard two magic words during Gus's woeful tale, and those words were: wall safe.

Manny Greenstreet had locked Gus's contract away in a safe—and most likely, the cash he'd taken from him as well. This might be a formidable barrier for most people, but not for me, and I decided I would help Gus out by using my finely honed criminal skills for good. The poor sucker. It was the least I could do.

With Gus snoring lightly, I went into the bedroom and changed out of the brown double-breasted suit that I'd worn to the club (along with my two-toned wingtips) and put on my 'work clothes': black slacks, black knitted turtleneck, and of course, my black crepe-soled shoes. I also wear a black leather A1 aviator jacket that dates back to the Great War. It hugs my waist and chest tight and has slashing zippered pockets that run down each side of my torso, as well as a couple of front pockets over my stomach with flaps that snap shut. The jacket is light and easy to maneuver in, and the various pockets come in handy for carrying my lock picks or for stashing loot.

I also grabbed my Dents, a pair of peccary driving gloves. Dents make the best gloves in the world. My pair has a keyhole back, knuckle holes, and aeration along the tops of the fingers. They are unlined, light, dexterous, and very expensive. And—as I'm pretty sure you've already guessed—they're black. I wear them faithfully on every job. As Pops would always say:

> *Leaving fingerprints is like leaving a calling card. You might as well send a personal invitation to the heat to come pick you up.*

I quietly stepped out of my bedroom and crouched near the wall separating the living room and kitchen, where an iron ornamental grate covers the cold air return. Inside the air shaft, above the tin flue, is a hollow space I created as a hiding spot. I use it to store contraband and small equipment that I use for my jobs. I also keep an extra bit of cash handy—just in case I ever need to take it on the lam. It's not my main stash spot—I use a locker down at Penn station for that—but the hole is big enough to hold the leather caddy that contains my lock picks and a small penlight.

I unscrewed the grate and retrieved the items I needed. Gus remained snoring and paid me no attention. However, 'Puff' had become curious and tried several times to explore inside the flue. So I grabbed him by the scruff of his neck and deposited him out through the fire-escape window. You can bet he'll be back tomorrow, but under a new assumed name.

I put my items in a zippered pocket and then left, quiet as a mouse, locking the apartment door behind me.

4

TWENTY MINUTES LATER, I was crossing Union Square. Traffic was light, with barely any pedestrians out at two-thirty in the morning. Looming across the way was the S. Klein department store—its windows dark and its doors shuttered for the evening.

I passed by the statue of the Marquis de Lafayette overlooking the Square from his pedestal of Quincy granite, his left hand extended palm up as if to welcome passersby—or maybe asking for a handout. Could be this damn depression we're in has hit the statuary world too. He was plum out of luck, however. Passing by, I didn't give him a red cent.

A bar on the corner showed some activity. It was past closing time, but a few drunk stragglers were bending the city rules. The owner was attempting to shove them out the door. They were boisterous and not quite ready for the night to end. Across the street three women huddled together, smoking, their lips slathered red with lipstick. Their dresses were tight and garish and designed to show off their wares. I could tell they weren't headed to church. They threw teasing waves towards the freshly booted men, who lustily crossed the street to keep the party alive. Fortunately, none of them noticed me slinking across the cityscape.

By the time I turned down the street to where Manny Greenstreet's office was located, I was alone—well, pretty much.

Half a block down, one fellow was limping toward me like he might have had too much to drink. Maybe he had been with the other drunks and got turned around. The moment I spotted him, I tried hugging the buildings, sticking to the shadows, but he must have caught sight of me because even in his drunken stupor, he hurriedly hobbled across the street to avoid me.

As we passed by on opposite sides of the street, I noticed him to be well-dressed, in a brown, three-piece suit and a homburg hat. A business man. He gripped his briefcase tight against his chest as if afraid I was going to take it from him. I couldn't blame him. Dressed in black like I was, I looked like a thug.

I chuckled. He made for a humorous sight. His night of revelry had left him in disarray. He had torn his jacket pocket open; it flapped against his thigh like a flag. But I kept my head down and averted, staring at him directly. As it was, I was trying to avoid him as much as he was me.

Once he turned the corner, the street became quiet. The only movement was a dog scrounging in an overturned garbage can next door. The mongrel lifted his nose to scrutinize me as I approached, but noticing that I was well-fed and not a competitor for his found treasure, he went back to rooting around.

I found Greenstreet's building in the middle of the block. A sign outside in red letters said: Knickerbocker Wrestling Federation. The building was on my side of the street, so I crossed over to the opposite side to get a better view. An abandoned building was across the way, its windows boarded up and the front door padlocked. I climbed the stoop to hide in the shadows of the recessed door frame and watched.

All the lights in the wrestling club building were out except one. It glowed in the window of a corner office four floors up. It concerned me at first, making me wonder if someone was inside. However, as I watched, no movement took place through the window and no shadows played on the ceiling that would indicate that anyone was in the office, so I figured someone had left the lights on by accident.

It didn't matter; I knew from Gus's tale that Manny Greenstreet's office was on the ground floor next to the gym. Even if someone occupied the building four stories up, they wouldn't be hearing me from there. I'm nearly soundless on the job.

Checking the street up and down, I found it clear. Even the dog had moved on. I was good to go.

I slipped across the street and stepped up to the front door. I took out my penlight and crouched to check the lock. It was an oldie, probably Victorian from the last century. It had a cast-iron rim lock with an oval logo that read: Logan-Gregg Sterling Hardware. I'd heard of them but had never come across one of their locks before. But that's okay, because I could see that the lock required a skeleton key, and that's my favorite kind of lock. They are so cute and useless.

From one of my zippered pockets, I retrieved the soft leather caddy that holds my lock-picks.

My lock-picks are my most cherished possessions. Pops had handcrafted them for me, meticulously shaping each one to perfection. He had given them to me as a gift a few weeks before being shot to death—my only inheritance.

The caddy holds an array of choice picks with slender wooden handles that are stained dark walnut. I have three different torsion wrenches, which are 'L' shaped, including a 'twist-flex' torsion. The rest are: a hook pick, a steep half diamond, a shallow half diamond, a snake rake, an 'S' rake, a double round, and several others I use to breach most modern locks.

However, this lock was not modern by any means.

No problem. Pops—being the thorough thief he was—had added a bonus gift: a separate ring containing eight different warded picks, which are thin and flat with various shapes at the end. I use them specifically as skeleton keys.

After giving the door frame a quick look for an alarm system and finding none, I had the door lock breached in twenty seconds. As I said, skeleton keys are my favorite.

On any job, the initial entry is the most exhilarating, however, the most dangerous too. You never know what lurks on the other side of a locked door. The room may be empty or occupied. A security guard could very well be waiting for you with a revolver trained on your mid-section, all because his sharp ears had picked up the scraping sound of you fiddling with the lock.

Or worse, there could be a dog. I hate dogs. And they tend to hate late-night intruders.

Taking in a breath, I twisted the handle and entered the Knickerbocker Wrestling Federation building.

5

No guards. No dogs.

Closing the door behind me, I stood dead still for a full two minutes, listening. Nothing stirred.

In front of me was a small, empty lobby. It was clean and dark, the only lights coming from a couple of sconces on the back wall. The interior design was turn-of-the-century, cheap, yet somewhat stylish. The floor tile had an art deco flair. Off to the right was a staircase leading upstairs, with a railing of twisted wrought iron spindles and a brass hand railing. They had installed a modern elevator across the way, which looked far more reliable than the one in my building.

To the left was a hallway leading deeper into the building. A placard on the wall showed that the Knickerbocker Wrestling Federation was to be found that way. So that is where I went.

At the end of the short hall was a set of double doors. Assuming them to be locked, I tried the handle, and it surprised me to find them unlocked. I let myself in.

Inside was a reception area for the wrestling club. It stood in stark difference to the lobby behind me. Ratty and musty smelling. The type of reception area you might find in an old filling station. It had a beat-up wooden desk, a few grimy chairs, and posters of girls in bathing suits pinned to the wall behind the desk. The left-hand wall displayed the local heroes of the sport, with about twenty framed photographs of wrestlers tacked up, some in costume, some not. No one I recognized. None of the photos were of Jim Londos, the Golden Greek—he wouldn't be caught dead in a place like this.

There was a door to the side of the desk, so I took it and found that it opened into another hall with a couple of offices on either side. The offices had wainscoting below and frosted glass above. I don't like frosted glass. The word *exposure* comes to mind. It requires you to keep the light inside at a minimum because it can be easily seen from outside.

The end of the hall opened up into a broad space with a high ceiling of crisscrossing I-beams. Even in the darkness, I could see that it was a gym. Ambient light bounced off the ropes of a wrestling ring set a couple of feet higher than the floor. I could make out backless benches set up around the ring, some of them overturned. Several used towels were strewn about and discarded handbill programs cluttered the floor. Must have been the maid's day off.

I didn't enter the gym, however, because I came to Manny Greenstreet's office first. Someone had hand-painted his name on the frosted glass, someone who was *not* a sign painter. Squatting down to check the door lock, I found it to be an old vertical rim-lock with a clay knob. And yep, my favorite kind of lock again—a skeleton key.

But giving the handle a twist, I found this door to be unlocked as well. My lucky day. Someone got sloppy closing up.

I stepped in.

Because of the frosted glass, I kept the lights off, just in case someone happened by.

The room stank, as if buckets of wrestling sweat had been poured over the walls and allowed to fester. It was so sour it hurt my lungs to breathe. I nearly backed out of the room at that moment just to get another breath of fresh air. However, I reasoned, it would do no good to waste time retreating at this point. Besides, even if I got a lungful of fresh air, I couldn't hold my breath the entire time it takes to crack a safe. That would be impossible! I needed to man up and take it. I'd come for that contract, dammit, and I was going to get it, even if it took scorching a few nostril hairs doing so.

As my eyes adjusted to the darkness, a shape formed in front of me that became further proof that I had Manny Greenstreet's office. The overturned office desk remained on its side from Gus's temper flare. It laid there in the middle of the room like a dying wildebeest. A couple of its legs were busted off—just as Gus had described. I couldn't see too clearly, it being dark and all, but I could tell that the place was a wreck, like a cyclone had hit it. I suppose it had—*The Storming Swede.*

But I wasn't here to tidy up, so I didn't.

I took out my penlight and flashed it against the right-hand wall. I spotted the safe immediately. I edged over and washed the penlight over it. It was flush to the wall, with a fourteen inch square face; it had a small dial and handle. I smiled when I recognized the make and model. Pasted in the corner was a red logo that read *Hercules*—which may sound formidable but is not. The manufacturer was Meilink, and they had designed this model to be more fireproof than burglar-proof—which works to my benefit.

I was about to give the dial a twirl to begin the work of cracking the combination when one of Pops' rules came to mind:

> *Always give a tug first. A lot of idiots own safes. And idiots sometimes forget to twirl the dial when locking up.*

I'd never come across a closed safe yet where this was the case, but I suppose there's always a chance of stumbling onto one. And so far tonight, the only door I had to breach was the self-locking front door. Someone had left the last two doors open.

I twisted the handle and...

...got the shock of my life. It turned! The safe was already unlocked.

Manny Greenstreet, apparently, was one of those idiots that Pops had made the rule about.

This was going to make my job a breeze. Cracking a safe can sometimes take hours—not for me, but for most. However, now I'd be in and out within minutes, like mere smoke passing through the night.

I opened the safe and stood there, dumbfounded by what I found.

I found it empty.

Disappointment slapped me in the face. Gus's contract wasn't there.

It also disappointed me on another level. I had hoped to find other valuables in the safe as well. Like cash. Yes, my primary goal was the contract (and possibly the dough Gus had lost to this character), but I'm not entirely altruistic. While I was here, I thought I might as well get paid for my efforts—not by Gus, but by Mr. Manny Greenstreet, thank-you.

Oh well. Pops always said:

> *Mysteries lie behind the closed doors of a safe. Sometimes treasure, sometimes dust. But it's always fun finding out which.*

I don't know, Pops. Finding dust isn't all that fun to me.

I also felt sorry for Gus. I was hoping to help him out of a jam. Get him on a bus back to St. Cloud. Reunite him with his family. Help facilitate his career goal of smacking around other corn-fed schmucks.

Then a thought occurred to me. Maybe the contract was still in the office somewhere. It wouldn't hurt to take a quick look around.

However, I needed more light. My penlight hadn't a strong enough beam for a thorough search.

Now, as I had mentioned, in offices with frosted glass, I hate turning on lights if I don't have too, but it being so late and the building so quiet, I figured it was probably safe enough to turn on a light for a brief minute or two—if I could find one. Maybe a desk lamp had been thrown to the floor when Gus had created havoc.

Turning around, I took a step toward the overturned desk and suddenly plummeted to the floor.

I'd tripped on something—something large!

My outstretched arms saved me from getting a face-full of floor.

But the penlight went flying. It spun across the tiled floor like a top, creating a flickering strobe effect in the room. The light came to rest eight feet away, with its beam shining in my face.

My heart was pounding from the surprise of it all. The clatter had been loud. In my ears, it had sounded like a falling avalanche. My thoughts jumped to that lighted window four stories up; I only hoped no one had heard the clamor.

Twisting around, I discovered the source of my fall, and it was as bad as it gets.

A man was lying on the floor, staring at me.

6

MY HEART JACK-HAMMERED AT the sight.

The man was dead—that much was obvious. The voltage gone from his staring eyes.

My other clue was the brain matter leaking out of an open gash in his head like lumpy gravy.

I nearly gagged.

Scrambling to my feet, panic surged as I backed away from the body.

This was not good. Not good at all. Being in the same room with an open safe is one thing; being in the same room with an open head wound is another thing altogether.

How could I have not noticed him sooner?

It had been the disorder of the room. The upheaval. The darkness. And my singular focus on the safe. It had all added up to a major oversight.

A dead man lying on the floor behind me!

Bending down, I picked up the penlight and combed the area where the body lay.

The man was contorted in angles that humans shouldn't be able to bend. Blood was everywhere. Not in pools, but in spatters, like someone had flicked a paintbrush dipped in crimson. An arc of it ran up the wall. On the other side of the body, where I had been standing a moment ago, I could see smears in the spatter on the floor, and a couple of footprints up against the corpse. In my ignorance, I must have stepped in the blood.

The man appeared to be around forty-five, but I couldn't say for sure because of the relaxed death-wilt in his face. Everything sagged. Although, there seemed to be a hint of surprise frozen there as well, with the whites of his eyes shining and his mouth gaping. He was bald on top, with a fringe of dark hair, matted with blood. A pair of wire-rimmed glasses lay on the floor a few feet away, one lens broken with bits gone.

Also lying there was a leg from the busted desk, smeared with blood and globs of stuff that I didn't want to think about.

Was it Manny Greenstreet? Possibly. It was his office. But I'd never met the man, so I couldn't say.

My heart was still thumping. I needed to get out immediately. But something made me hesitate.

Even though Gus's contract seemed like a trivial matter suddenly, it still nagged at me. If it was here in the room, it wouldn't hurt to give a quick look around. After all, the man on the floor would not object—he hadn't so far.

I played the beam of my penlight around the floor. A bank style desk lamp was laying up against the wall, its bulb shattered. That's okay. I did not want to turn on a light at this point. Nothing to draw attention to the room. Even if it was nearly three in the morning and the building was empty.

For the place being a wreck, I didn't see any papers lying about—almost as if someone had picked up after themselves. Obviously, whoever had killed this man had also taken the items from the safe and any other papers of interest. Possibly there were items under the desk, but I wasn't about to turn it over and search there. As it was, I felt I was lingering far too long at a murder scene.

I decided to leave, and was turning to go, when something caught my eye. A sliver of white poked from under the jacket sleeve of the body. I crouched low to the floor to examine it. It was paper. However, it looked too small to be a contract and the ply too thick—like card stock.

Had the killer left his calling card? That would be rich.

Gently, I pulled it from beneath the fabric of the man's jacket. I ran the penlight over it. A few blood spatters had seeped along one edge, but not much. And it wasn't a calling card, but a ticket stub.

I could easily read the black lettering. It was for a train ticket, for the 20th Century Limited, a train that traveled from LaSalle Street Station in Chicago to Grand Central Terminal here in New York. I read the date, and for a brief second I thought it was for today, but then realized that—being three in the morning—it was really for yesterday evening. Arriving about 10:45.

I stood, holding the stub in my gloved hand, wondering about it. Was it Manny Greenstreet's ticket? Doubtful. From Gus's story, Manny hadn't been traveling this week, so it had to be someone else's. Had the killer left it? It couldn't have been lying on the floor for too long, for the date stamp was for last night. Possibly, someone had traveled from Chicago specifically to come to kill Manny Greenstreet—if indeed that was him on the floor.

Then a thought hit me like a baseball bat—or like a busted leg from a desk.

Gus.

He had arrived by train from Chicago—he told me so himself.

Was this his ticket stub?

I shriveled a little inside. I didn't want to think that Gus could have done in Manny Greenstreet. The kid seemed so...wholesome. A dupe from the sticks. But what did I know about Gustave Nordstrom?

When I'd come upon him last night, he was still pretty sore over the lousy way he'd been treated. Steaming with anger. He also appeared extremely distraught. He had just come from this very office, or—if you were to believe his story—*thrown* from this very office.

As much as I couldn't see it, I had to wonder: had Gus murdered Manny Greenstreet? Had he conned me? Had he fed me a sob story?

He certainly had a motive. Greenstreet had taken all his money and had crippled his fighting career with a binding contract.

He had opportunity—having been here a few hours ago, by his own admission.

And he had the means. A table leg taken from the desk—which he had overturned in fury.

Had I been doing a favor for a murderer?

The heck with it. I suddenly wanted nothing to do with this. If the contract was somewhere in the mess on the floor, so be it. Let the rube from Minnesota—*The Storming Swede*—figure it out.

I hesitated, biting my lower lip.

But what about the ticket stub? It was evidence. Should I leave it here? Let the police discover it? If the ticket belonged to Gus, it could help lead them to him pretty quick—and possibly to me, a thought I didn't care for. However, if it wasn't Gus's ticket, they still might use it to connect him to the murder, anyway. What should I do?

I slipped the ticket stub into one of my zippered pockets. I would deal with it later.

Carefully backing away from the body, I stepped around the desk, leaving the opposite way from how I came into the room. I wanted to avoid stepping in blood again. I could only imagine the trail of evidence I was leaving behind as it is. Being a criminal, I'm familiar with *Locard's Exchange Principle*, that a perpetrator of a crime will bring something to the crime scene and take something from it. I wasn't the perpetrator in this case, but I could still be leaving a trail of bread crumbs—and with the ticket stub in my pocket, I was certainly taking something from the scene!

My only saving grace was that there was little, or no, chance of this crime being traced back to me personally. Until a few hours ago, I had never heard of Manny Greenstreet and had no reason to be in this room, and nobody could prove otherwise. Maybe it was a good thing that the safe had been empty. The items inside would've only compounded the potential evidence trail that could've led to me.

I made it to the door without fainting and slipped into the hall, locking the door behind me. The warehouse gym remained deathly quiet. I rushed down the hall as fast as my legs could trot and into the front lobby. I exited through the front door and locked it. Hanging in the shadows of the recessed entryway for a moment, I scanned the length of the street for cars and pedestrians. Nothing stirred. Even the dog that had been nosing around in the garbage was nowhere to be seen.

I can't tell you how refreshing the New York night air smelled—yes, New York City air! It was as if I were a newborn breathing for the first time.

That's when it dawned on me.

That putrid smell I'd encountered when first entering the office. It hadn't been sweat at all. It had been the smell of death.

Manny Greenstreet's death.

Gus was still sleeping when I got back to the apartment. Ambient light from the city streamed through the front bay window. I stood in the darkness watching as he snored like a kitten, his chest rising and falling under the blanket. I'd been thinking about him on the way back and how I should handle the situation. Earlier, he hadn't seemed threatening to me at all, just pitiful, but now...

Who was this Gus, anyway? Yeah, he'd told me his story, and yeah, I'd bought it hook, line, and sinker, but had he told me the truth? The whole truth?

I now had some added information, and the facts appeared fairly explicit.

Gus was a big guy—at least six/two, and he had to weigh a couple of bucks, maybe more.

When I'd found him on the bench earlier this evening, he simmered with rage. He nearly bit my head off for simply saying hello.

He also had been scuffed up. Torn jacket and trousers. Bruised face. Scraped hands.

And bloody.

Blood on his fists. On his jacket sleeve. On his trousers. Not a lot. But enough. Spatters.

But I had seen spatters in Manny's office as well. Rooster tail spatters decorating the walls with blood.

Sure, Gus gave a reason for being blood-sopped. Five professional wrestlers had beat on him and kicked him to the street. But had that been true? The way he told it, it sounded plausible. Heck, the kid had such a home-spun honesty about him, anything coming from his mouth sounded plausible. But was it?

It came down to this basic question: can a home-spun boy from the Midwest beat to death a New York fight promoter?

I could picture it, but I couldn't picture it.

Being a thief, and the son of a thief—who was also one of the craftiest con-men in the city—I have a nose for deception. I can smell a scam, or a lie, a mile away. And I hadn't sniffed one this time. At the beginning of the evening, my gut had told me that Gus's story was legitimate. It felt genuine. If not, then he was one terrific tale weaver.

And if that was the case, this sleeping choir-boy I was looking at was a certified psychopathic liar…and possibly a murderer.

And what did I do? I invited him into my apartment, fed him, gave him a place to conk out—and then, stupidly, traipsed through his bloody crime scene.

What had I gotten myself into?

I went to my room, shutting the door lightly. I wanted to lock it, but couldn't. The door has no lock. Who needs to lock your bedroom door when you live alone? So I wrestled my dresser in front of it as an implausible blockade. Pretty paltry. A guy Gus's size would be through that barrier like busting through a wet newspaper. But it was all I had.

I turned on my lamp and stripped off my 'work clothes', inspecting each item in the light as I did. It surprised me to find that the blood transfer was minimal. I had a small smear on my pants on the shin of the right leg, where I had tumbled onto the body, but that was it. There was nothing on my aviator jacket; thank goodness—it's irreplaceable.

And my hands must have landed out of reach of the blood spatter perimeter because the Dents were completely free of blood. Peccary gloves are quite expensive and they take some time to break in. I was grateful that I wouldn't be throwing them away.

I held my shoes up to the light. Nothing on the top. Turing them over, I found the bottoms were clean too—absolutely clean. This surprised me the most, as I felt for sure that I had probably slipped on the blood spatter. Maybe I had been wrong. Maybe the shoe prints I'd seen at the scene hadn't been mine, but by the killer's. Or possibly, the blood wore off on the walk home.

Just to be sure, I took everything into the bathroom and scrubbed them down.

I then laid down on the bed and tried to sleep. It wasn't easy. I kept expecting the bedroom door to burst open and the raging murderer in the next room to come swooping in to attack me.

With no mercy.

Even after he had eaten all my bologna and cheese.

I AWOKE A FEW hours later to clatter coming from the next room. I leaped from my bed, startled by it, until my sleep-addled mind broke through the fog to remember my guest—you know, the possible murderer.

I grabbed my robe, moved my dresser away from the door and back into place, and went to see what all the noise was about.

I found Gus in the kitchen, down on his haunches and rooting through my cupboards. He glanced up as I stepped around the corner. His battered face flushed red when he saw me.

"Hey," he said, looking sheepish for being caught nosing around. "I was looking for a coffee pot. Thought I would have hot coffee ready for when you woke up."

I stared at him for a moment, wondering if I was looking at a wholesome young hick or a blood-thirsty maniac. "I don't have one," I said.

He looked surprised. "You don't drink coffee?"

"I didn't say that. I said I don't have a coffee pot. I always go down to Whitey's Place for my morning coffee. It's a diner a few blocks from here."

"Oh."

An awkward pause hung between us for a moment. He stood up to full height. Yeah, he was a big boy, at least six/two and over two hundred pounds. Wielding a desk leg would be mere batting practice for him.

After another awkward pause, I said, "I'll get dressed and we'll get some breakfast at Whitey's."

"I don't take charity," he replied, folding his arms defiantly.

"That's what you told me last night. And I said you could pay me back when you get back on your feet."

I turned toward the bedroom, but paused to look him over. He still wore the same clothes he'd slept in. Even the jacket.

"You got any other clothes? You look pretty shabby."

He looked down at himself as if he hadn't realized his condition. "I've got another shirt and a pair of dress slacks in my suitcase." He nodded toward the cardboard case he'd dragged in with him.

"How about another jacket?" I asked cautiously. "I noticed you got a bit of blood on the sleeves...down by the wrists."

He glanced at his cuffs. "Yeah, I guess I did." He chuckled. "I didn't even notice."

I took a small step forward, but not batting practice close. "And tell me again how you got blood on your jacket?"

He shrugged. "Musta happened when I fought those five guys at Mr. Greenstreet's place. I got some good licks in. Gave one of them a bloody nose. Busted one guy's jaw. I could feel it. Gave him a solid uppercut. And I'm pretty sure I busted another guy's ribs. I heard 'em crack." He grinned at the achievement.

"Uh-huh."

The guy seemed to think violence was pretty cute. We looked at each other some more. I glanced down at his shoes. There appeared to be a drop of blood or two on the toe of his right shoe, but nothing more. But then, I couldn't see the bottom of the soles either. They could've been smeared red.

The silence was growing beyond awkward, so I said:

"I doubt any of my jackets would fit you. Your shoulders are too big."

He shrugged. "That's okay. I don't mind looking like this if you don't."

"I'll get dressed." And turned to go to my room.

I took a shower, shaved, and got dressed. I put on my gray windowpane suit with the short peaked lapels and knotted up a light violet tie with black stripes. Being a warm day, I didn't bother with the vest. I wore my black oxfords—no crepes and no two-tones today.

I then gave Gus a turn in the shower. He didn't even argue with me about it. After three days and nights on the streets, he knew he needed one as much as the rest of us knew he needed one. He dressed in his dress slacks and a fresh shirt, and except for his battered face, didn't look half bad, even with his tattered and soiled jacket.

As we left the apartment, I grabbed my dark gray hat with the black Petersham ribbon. Gus wore the same herringbone newsy cap he had on when I found him.

Twelve minutes later we were walking through the door of Whitey's Place.

———◆———

9

BUILT BY THE FODERO Dining Car Company, Whitey's is a stainless steel structure of sleek horizontal lines and curved corners shaped like a train car. The architectural style is *art moderne*. I know this because Whitey himself told me. He's full of useless information like that. Whitey can talk about almost anything and sound pretty smart doing it. He made a point of stressing the 'durn' at the end of the word *moderne*, to signify that his establishment was classy and urbane. He told me all this while burning an order of sausages—urbane sausages of the *art moderne* style.

Whitey was a good friend of Pops, although he never knew about him being a thief. When Pops got shot to death, Whitey figured it was because Pops had been drunk and had stumbled into the wrong house by accident—even though we lived in Manhattan and Brooklyn was across the river. He also never believed the newspaper articles written about Pops being a burglar, thinking that the reporter must have gotten Pops mixed up with some other fella.

Whitey is the smartest man I know, but sometimes he's not so bright. However, he has a heart of gold, and when I was on my own years ago, he let me stay at his place off and on.

As we came through the door, the white Bakelite radio that sits on the shelf by the door was playing *Dancing in the Moonlight*, by Ruth Etting. She was telling us to:

Give a boy a June night, Give a girl a song, They'll be dancing in the moonlight all night long.

The place was half full, with a mid-morning crowd. But for some reason, all the customers were packed into the booths at the far right end of the diner, leaving the left side empty, including all the stools at the counter. It felt strange, as if half the diner was under an evacuation order. Although I must admit, the crowd squished together down there appeared lively and full of smiles.

I shrugged at the sight and led Gus to a booth at the empty end. I wanted privacy anyway. There were some pointed questions I wanted to ask him, and the fewer ears, the better.

Trudy, one of the waitresses, leaned an elbow on the customer-less counter near us. Her other hand was fisted and propped on her ample hip. A cigarette wiggled between her bright pink lips. She was glaring at the crammed booths at the far of the diner with a shrewd, detached eye. She looked peeved.

Trudy is a Whitey's icon. I can adequately describe her as roly-poly. Her face is as round as a dinner plate with rosy cheeks and fake eyelashes as long as a child's finger. She dyes her bushy hair fireplug red, and always stores a couple of pencils in it, which stick out like missiles ready to be launched. She's a brash, gum-snapping woman, who swears like a sailor, always has an available dirty joke to share, and flirts ruthlessly with the customers. Everyone is called 'hon' or 'sweetie'.

She also has a temper. I once saw her throw an iron skillet—with a rash of bacon sizzling inside—at a fry cook for pinching her butt. Knocked him out cold.

As we slid into a booth overlooking the street, Trudy seemed oblivious to our presence. I gave a slight rap on the table and she swiveled, what I interpreted to be, an annoyed look our way.

"Oh!" she exclaimed, almost surprised to see us. She stood upright and stamped out her cigarette in an ashtray on the counter. A fabricated smile hit her dinner plate face. "Morning, Hun. You boys want coffee? A fresh pot is brewing. I'll get some cups and be right with you." And she toddled off around the counter.

As we waited, I looked Gus over. He stared through the window. His blue mid-western eyes appeared mesmerized by the bustle of the city. Even with his mug all black and blue, he had the shine of innocence, like a big teddy bear come to life. A murdering teddy bear? Hard to believe, but maybe.

"I know I've only been here for four days now," he said wistfully, "but I can't get used to how big this city is. It makes St. Cloud look like a corn field. Everyone seems to be rushing somewhere. Where is everyone going all dressed up?"

"Jobs. People have to work," I offered.

Turning toward me, he looked a bit awe-faced. "Of course, I should have thought of that. I don't suppose there are many farmers in Manhattan."

"No. Not many."

"Where do you work, Buck? I never asked last night. Don't you have a job to go to today?"

I hesitated. Normally, I have a spiel about being in the antiquities market (I procure them for clients, I say—a.k.a. fences, but I always leave that part out). But I couldn't bring myself to lie to this kid. It was that genuine mug of his. It would be like lying to a priest.

Fortunately, Trudy appeared at our table, pouring coffee into cups, and sparing me from my moral dilemma.

"Fresh pot of jo to get your blood perking," she said between gum snaps. Her tone was suddenly cheery, but it felt forced and over the top. "How's my favorite customer doing today, Buck? You look good enough to eat." She chomped her teeth at me and winked. She then turned to take in Gus. "Stop the presses. What kind of man-flesh do we have here? Is this your first time at Whitey's, Sweetums?"

Gus grinned, "Yes, ma'am."

"Ma'am?" She recoiled with fake shock, then poked me with an elbow. "Look at the manners on this one. You're not from around here, are you, honey?"

Gus shook his head.

"What happened to your face, darling? You get hit by a bus?"

He shrugged. "Something like that."

"Aw, you poor thing. You're a good-looking kid under all those bruises." She eyed him with a toothy grin and gave a stroke of his cheek with the back of her hand. "Yes sir, you're a big hunky kid. A gorgeous piece of man flesh, you are!"

Gus gulped. His face nearly turned the color of Trudy's hair, his bruises purpling.

"What's your name, Sweetums?" She asked, setting the carafe down and pulling an order pad from her apron.

"Gus."

"I knew a Gus once. Boy, did I show him some tricks." She grabbed a pencil from her hair. "He had trouble walking after. I could show them to you too, sweetie."

Gus shuddered in embarrassment, or repulsion, hard to tell.

I quickly interrupted, "I think we'll just take breakfast, Trudy, and leave the tricks for another day."

She laughed, throwing her head back. "Suit yourself. But taking a ride on Trudy's Bump and Grunt can be life changing."

Gus withered in his seat.

Trudy wrote down our orders. As she stuck her pencil back into her hair, I asked:

"Hey Trudy, what's with the convention at the other end of the diner?"

Her lip curled into a sneer. "You mean pervert alley?"

I gave her a questioning squint, and she shot me a warning glare. Her finger was suddenly in my face.

"Don't you dare move to a booth at that end, Buck Flynn! I've got your food coming right here." She waved her order pad and then slammed it against the table's edge.

I blinked at her response. "Whoa, we're not moving anywhere."

"Yeah, you say that now, but—"

"But what? Why would we move?"

She scowled.

"What?"

Suddenly, at the other end of the counter, the kitchen doors swung open, and I understood fully.

A girl entered carrying an armload of hot platters. And what a girl! A stunning beauty. She wore little make-up, but had a Mediterranean glow that certainly didn't require it. With creamy skin of light caramel that hinted of being perpetually tan, she possessed high cheek-bones and dark, exotic eyes. Her ebony hair was thick and wavy, stylishly pinned back under the curved waitress hat, and she wore a small red rose over her right ear. The pink waitress uniform snugged an hourglass figure and, even while carrying food, she strolled across the checkered tile floor like a starlet stepping onto a set.

And what a stroll! Ocean waves came to mind.

The customers at the other end, as a unit, immediately perked to attention in their seats. That's when I realized something I hadn't noticed before—they were all male. The crowd almost cheered her arrival.

She was stop-the-music gorgeous.

"Will you look at that," I said, my voice catching. Behind me, I was pretty sure I heard Gus audibly gulp.

"Meet the new waitress," muttered Trudy bitterly. "All the pervs want to sit at her tables."

"I can't see why," I lied. My eyes were studying the contours of the new girl's uniform. Trudy wore the same style, pink with a white apron. Trudy's uniform had contours too, but it was hard to believe that both garments came from the same manufacturer. They stretched over the two women with entirely different purposes.

As if reading my thoughts, Trudy cuffed the backside of my head, knocking my hat off.

"Ow...that hurt," I cried.

"You're not moving! Your food is coming to this table. And your tip had better be on this table too! You're the first customers I've had in forty-five minutes."

She turned and stomped off.

Gus smirked as he handed me back my hat. "Guess she told you."

I frowned as I rubbed the back of my head. "Strange way to ask for a tip, if you ask me," I offered.

———◦———

10

THE NEW WAITRESS SASHAYED back into the kitchen. In her passing, the doors swung open again and a new form stepped through. The sight rather disappointing in comparison.

It was Whitey himself.

He planted his short, stocky body in the middle of the aisle with his hands akimbo on his hips, giving a curious squint at the lopsided displacement of patrons in his establishment. He scratched his head in wonderment, as if he had no clue as to explain such a phenomenon. A chorus of hoots and hellos resounded from that end of the diner. One fellow stood and raised his coffee cup.

"To Whitey," he yelled. "A man with an eye for talent."

The men broke out in laughter.

Whitey threw them a dismissive wave and, shaking his head, turned to come our way.

"Do you believe those animals?" he said as he approached. "I thought I'd better come join you guys before the combined weight at that end breaks through the floor and into the subway."

I moved over so he could take a seat and introduced him to Gus. They shook hands.

Whitey is the fun uncle everyone has in their family tree. Built as solid as a brick chimney, his affable manner makes it seem you've always known him, and you can't help but like him immediately. His hair line may have given up years ago, but his smile is broad and his eyes glint with mischief and a hint of wisdom. His outfit rarely varies, dark slacks, white-shirt—always with the rolled-up sleeves to expose a couple of tattoos he inherited during a stint in the Navy—and a bow tie.

"New waitress, huh?" I said cautiously, watching to make sure that Trudy, with her cuffing hand, was out of reach.

"Yeah, a great kid. Her name's Rosy. Her full name is Rosalina Genovese—Italian. I know her father. We were in the Navy together."

"Rosalina Genovese," I said. "Kind of rolls right off your tongue in a musical way, doesn't it?"

Whitey chuckled. "I guess, but she wants us all to call her Rosy Grace."

"Why's that?"

"She's trying to become an actress. Rosy Grace is her stage name."

I turned to look over my shoulder as she came through the doors again. "Yeah, I'd pay to see that."

"You're paying to see that now," said Whitey with his broad grin. "And it comes with a meal too."

He turned to face Gus.

"So you're from Minnesota, Gus? What brings you to town?"

Gus looked chagrined, as if too embarrassed to explain. "I came to here to box, sir, but it looks like I'm gonna end up being a wrestler instead."

"Oh?" said Whitey, nodding at this information with something of admiration. "I enjoy watching wrestling. But you don't seem too happy about it."

"Not so much. They want me to take a dive for a few matches before they let me start winning. I don't like the idea of that."

Both of Whitey's hands came up to slap either side of his face in fake surprise. "Are you telling me they rig wrestling matches? I am shocked! Shocked, to learn this absolutely new information."

The act almost made Gus smile. "Yeah, I guess."

"Wait a minute," I said. "You know the matches are phony and you still like to watch them?"

"Sure," said Whitey with a shrug. "It's fun."

"But it's fake."

"So what? My wife drags me to watch plays on Broadway all the time. They're fake too. We watched a murder mystery the other night and I'm gonna tell you a secret..." He leaned over and whispered with a cuffed hand near his mouth, "...no one actually got killed."

I nodded. "I guess I hadn't thought of it that way."

"So Gus, why so gloomy? I'm guessing you don't want to be a wrestler," said Whitey.

Gus sighed.

"He kind of got caught in the ol' switcheroo," I interjected. "A promoter tricked him into signing a contract before he knew what was in it. They want him to wear a Viking costume."

Gus slumped just hearing me say it.

"I'm sorry to hear that," said Whitey. "I enjoy watching wrestling, but I admit it's changed since I was a kid. Back in the day, the bouts authentic, with real wrestlers, no acting. Those guys were brutes. I saw the first match between Frank Gotch and George Hackenschmidt in Chicago in 1908."

Whitey smiled proudly at this statement. But Gus and I must have looked bewildered, because he quickly deflated, realizing we had no idea what he was talking about.

"Oh, come on! Are you guys telling me you've never heard of Frank Gotch?"

"You do realize that 1908 was six years before I was born," I said.

"So! Read a history book, for crying out loud. Gotch was one of the greatest athletes of his time. He was the World Heavyweight Wrestling Champion for half a decade. And he trained with none other than Farmer Burns."

Again with the stupid looks.

"You guys are hopeless," said Whitey, shaking his head. "Farmer Burns was a pioneer in wrestling at the turn of the century. He was in nearly six thousand wrestling matches and only lost seven of them."

"Wow," said Gus. "Six thousand matches. He must've wrestled every night of his life."

"And get this, even though Burns was the American Heavyweight Champion, he only weighed a hundred and sixty pounds. He started up a wrestling school in Iowa. He's the one who trained Frank Gotch."

"The guy you saw in 1908," I offered.

"That's right. Anyway, there was this character from Europe, a powerful wrestler named, George Hackenschmidt, called the *Russian Lion*. He was undefeated with all comers. You should've seen this guy. His muscles had baby muscles that grew up to have more babies. It looked like he had automobile tires under his skin. Huge. So my father takes me to watch this match between him and Frank Gotch at the Dexter Park Pavilion in '08. It was something. They were at each other for two hours, both of them on their feet, before Gotch trapped him up against the ropes."

Whitey was now playing the role of both wrestlers, squirming in his seat and grappling with imaginary arms and legs, twisting them with pretzel-like motions. During the story, Trudy stopped by to refill our coffee cups, squinted at her boss's pantomime, and walked away, shaking her head.

"And finally, Gotch took him down. He got The Lion in a toe-hold, which was Gotch's signature move. His toe-hold could cripple a guy."

I almost expected Whitey's shoe to make an appearance at the table, but thankfully, it did not.

"The Lion couldn't outdo the toe hold. Gotch was an expert at it. So The Lion quit the fall. That round went to Gotch. They both retired to their locker rooms to take a break for—"

"Wait a minute," cried Gus, interrupting. "They were at it for two hours and it wasn't over?"

Whitey gave a wave. "Naw. They were supposed to come back out for the second fall, but Hackenschmidt refused to leave the locker room. He was done. Told the referee that he didn't want to wrestle anymore. They declared Gotch the winner. The place exploded."

During his tale, sweat had come to pepper his bald head. He took out his handkerchief and mopped his brow as he stood up.

"Yep, those were the days of real wrestling. Of real men."

He turned to saunter off, his shoulders a tad more square than when he'd sat down.

"That Whitey is some character," said Gus. "He reminds me of my uncle Floyd."

I nodded. "Yeah, he reminds everyone of their uncle somebody."

Gus looked cheery for the first time since meeting him. I hated to pop his bubble, but it was time for some pointed questions. I needed to know if I was buying breakfast for a killer.

11

I FOLDED MY HANDS around my coffee cup and leaned across the table.

"Gus, now that we got a minute alone, I need to ask a few questions about what happened to you last night."

"I already told you what happened."

"I know. I just want to get it straight."

He shrugged. "Go ahead."

"When you went back to Greenstreet's office last night, what time was that?"

He thought for a moment. "About ten-thirty or eleven."

I flashed on the arrival time stamped on the train ticket that I'd found. The train had come in at 10:45. "Did you go straight there from the train station?"

He gave a bewildered squint. "Why would I be at the train station?"

"You told me you came in by train."

"Yeah, three days ago—uh, wait...four days ago now. No, I'd just been wandering the streets. Don't ask me where. I couldn't tell you. It's easy to get lost in this city. But I still had the address for the wrestling gym, so I went back last night. I wanted to catch him after the wrestling show."

"They had a wrestling show last night?"

"That's right. They held it down at the gym. That was the show where he wanted me to take a dive."

I watched his face for signs of deception. None. I also recalled, from my visit to the gym last night, the scene of the arena, and how the benches were set up around the stage and the discarded programs on the floor. It must have been the remnants of the show.

"Were you alone when you met with Greenstreet at his office?"

A curious glint struck his eyes. "Why do you want to know that?"

"I just want to picture the scene in my mind."

"Why?"

"I'm trying to think of a way to get you out of a jam."

"Whadda ya mean?"

"The contract that you signed. I thought maybe I could help."

"You mean help me get out of it somehow?"

"Something like that. What does Manny Greenstreet look like?"

"Short guy. Has a bit of a gut. He's bald on top and wears glasses."

Yep...that sounded like the guy on the floor.

"So, was anyone else in the office when you met with him?"

"Yeah, his business partner, a guy named Mr. Jacobs."

"Does he have a first name?"

"I'm thinking it was, Mickey. At least that's what I heard Mr. Green-street call him."

Mickey Jacobs. The name sounded familiar, but I couldn't quite place it.

"Some girl was there too, wearing a nurse's outfit."

"Well, I suppose they need to have medical staff on hand in case a wrestler gets hurt."

He let out a laugh. "Hardly. She was one of the wrestlers—she just dresses like a nurse."

I gave a start, blinking. "A girl wrestler?"

"Yeah, sounds dumb, doesn't it? But I guess guys pay to watch girls beat each other up. Can you imagine that?"

Yeah, I could imagine it. "Was she a pretty girl?"

"I guess she was pretty...in the face. Nothing like..." His eyes drifted toward the other end of the diner. I turned around to glance that way. The new waitress was bending over a table pouring coffee. When I looked back,

Gus was a little slack-jawed. I gave a sharp rap on the table and he shook his head, as if coming out of a trance. "Uh...what was I saying?"

"You were saying that the girl in the nurse's outfit was pretty."

"Oh, right. She was. But she's also built like a guy. All muscle. I think her name is Flo."

"Tell me about this Jacobs fella—the business partner."

"Not much to tell. I only met him twice. The first day I got into town and then again last night. He's a big guy, about my height. And from the way he carries himself, I'm thinking he was a fighter at one time—or maybe a wrestler."

"Did he try to stop you when you started throwing the desk around?"

Gus's eye brightened. "Come to think of it, no. He started laughing like he thought it was funny. I got the impression that he and Mr. Greenstreet weren't chummy, if you know what I mean."

"What made you think that?"

"The first day I got there...on Tuesday, I walked into the office in the middle of an argument. Mr. Jacobs, the big guy, was calling Mr. Greenstreet a putz. Say...what is a putz?"

"A jerk."

"Oh."

"What was the fight about?"

"I dunno. I just got off the train half an hour earlier. I was just happy to be standing and not sitting."

"Did you take the Twentieth Century Limited?"

"Naw. I took the Lake Shore Limited. Tickets were cheaper."

Seemed like a plausible answer. But until I could prove it, he wasn't quite off the hook yet.

"Did this Mickey Jacobs fella seem like the violent type?" I asked.

"He was the bully type. I could tell that right away."

"How's that?"

"Well, I could tell that Mr. Greenstreet was a little afraid of him. I see guys like Mr. Jacobs around the gym back home all the time. Big guys, who like to tower over smaller guys and act intimidating. He was like one of them. Me...I don't need to push around smaller guys to prove myself...I just let my fists do the talking."

I didn't know if I liked the sound of that. "Did Jacobs join in with the other wrestlers to help throw you out?"

"You mean, did he help the other five guys? Naw. He sat in the corner and laughed his face off. He thought it was funny."

Trudy arrived with our food and placed it in front of us. She flashed Gus a seductive wink and added an air kiss. He shriveled into the booth.

After she left, he said, "I wish she wouldn't do that. She's old enough to be my mother."

"Trudy's old enough to be Noah's mother." I dug into my eggs. "Tell me what happened just before you turned the desk over."

"I told you already. Mr. Greenstreet waved the contract in my face. Called me a stupid rube. Said he owned me."

"Why did he still have it?"

"Whadda ya mean?"

"The contract. Why hadn't he taken it to his lawyer yet? He must have had it for three days."

"Oh, I see what you mean. He told me his lawyer was out of town for a few days. After he put it in the safe, he smirked at me and told me his lawyer was due back in town and he was going to run it up to his office first thing in the morning. That's when I got mad." Gus gave a sheepish smile. "And went a little berserk, I suppose."

I took a sip of coffee and asked the next question very casually. "Did he spin the dial?"

He paused in mid-bite, hash brown potatoes suspended near his lips. "Spin the dial? What dial?"

"The dial to the safe?"

He blinked. "What kind of question is that?"

"I'm just curious. Thought it might mean something."

"Like what?"

"I dunno, something. Did he spin or not?"

"I don't know if he spun the dial or not, I—wait! He did spin it. I remember now. 'Cause, that's when he smirked at me—right after he did it. He twisted the dial with flair. Like he was mocking me, like he was saying: try to get it now!"

"Hmm," I murmured, thinking it over in my mind. That meant someone re-opened the safe after Gus left, and then closed it again, but failed to lock it, because I found it open. "Do you think this Jacobs character knows the combination to the safe?"

"How the heck should I know?" He leaned in. "Wait. Are you thinking that we should go down and ask Mr. Jacobs to open the safe for us so we can get that contract back? 'Cause I doubt he will. He and Mr. Greenstreet may not like one another, but they're still partners. I'm sure he's not about to tear up my contract."

I wasn't thinking that at all. I was thinking that he might have been the one to open the safe later in the evening, but I wasn't about to tell Gus that.

Gus glanced at his wristwatch. "Besides, it's already after nine. Mr. Greenstreet said he would take the contract up to his lawyer's office first thing in the morning. It's probably already there."

I watched him deflate and slump in his seat, pushing his plate away.

"That's it. My boxing life is over. I guess I'm a wrestler now."

"Hey, don't give up yet. We still might be able to—" I stopped in mid-sentence. Something caught my eye outside the diner window. Something that raised the hackles on my neck.

An unmarked squad car had just pulled up to the curb in front of Whitey's.

"What's wrong?" asked Gus. "You look like you've seen a ghost."

I said nothing, watching as the plain-clothes officer got out of the vehicle. I recognized him immediately. Sergeant Detective Wilbur Crenshaw. My nemesis.

Crenshaw has dogged me relentlessly over the years. He knew my Pops back in the day and had dogged him too. He has never caught me in any crime yet—not even for violating a 'keep off the grass' sign—but it's not for lack of trying. He can be a royal pain in the neck.

The sight of him made me nervous, making me wonder why he was here. Was it just to eat breakfast? Have coffee? Or maybe he'd heard about the new waitress and decided to swing by perv alley to ogle some.

My wondering didn't last long.

He wasn't here for breakfast, or to leer at the new waitress. As he slammed shut the cruiser door, his eyes swept the length of the diner, combing the interior through the smoke-glassed windows. He stopped abruptly the moment he found me staring back at him.

A cunning smile broke across his ugly face and he lifted his hand to shoot a finger gun my way.

His way of telling me to stay put...and that he had me in his sights.

———◆———

12

I CALLED WILBUR UGLY, but to be fair, a better description would be goofy. He has a gnomish quality about him, small-boned and hunched. He looks like Jimmy Durante without the joy. And though he may look goofy, he's not. He's a sly fox with a sharp mind. And a persistent predator.

His sudden presence indicated that he had been looking for me. I could tell. The question was: Why?

The words, trace evidence, took a taunting jaunt through my mind.

"What's wrong, Buck?" asked Gus again, breaking my thoughts.

I leaned over and spoke in a quick whisper. "Look, Gus, a cop is coming our way. He's going to be asking questions. Say as little as possible."

"What do you mean?"

"I mean, don't volunteer any information. Don't tell him why you're in town or how you got here. And mention nothing about knowing Manny Greenstreet or being near the Knickerbocker Wrestling Federation—unless he asks. And whatever you do, don't say a word about getting mad and throwing the desk around."

"Why?"

"Just do what I say and—"

The bell above the jamb tinkled like a warning siren as Detective Crenshaw came through the door. I went quiet the second he appeared. Crenshaw gave a sweeping surveillance of the dinner, squinting curiously at the crowd jammed into the booths at the one end. He appeared baffled by it, but then shrugged and turned to head straight for our booth.

As he came our way, he gave Trudy a wave. She flashed him a wink in return—which looked a bit conspiratorial to me, like maybe she'd tipped him off to my being here. But maybe not. She winks at everybody. I didn't want to think of Trudy as being a rat. Lusty, yes. Rat, no.

"Hello Bucky," he said through clenched teeth as he drew up to our table.

I mentioned before that only one person on the planet gets away with calling me Bucky, and this is the guy. Not much I can do about it.

"You have the plague today?" he asked. He gave a thumb jerk toward the other end of the dinner. "Or is everyone wising up and keeping their distance from you?"

"New waitress," I said.

His head swiveled around just as Rosy Grace came through the doors carrying platters of food.

"Oh..." he croaked, staring. "Yeah, she is new."

His eyes dawdled over Rosy Grace for a moment before snapping his attention back to me.

"I thought I would catch you here—when I couldn't find you at your apartment."

He gave a wave of his fingers Gus's way, a gesture instructing him to shove over so he could take a seat. He then slipped into the booth next to him. He gave Gus a cursory glance, which told me he wasn't here for Gus, but for me, yet did a double-take once he spotted the bruises on his face. He recoiled a bit and grew a bit more inquisitive.

"Who are you?" he asked.

"Gustave Nordstrom, sir," replied Gus. He offered the detective his hand.

"Sir? Did you hear that, Bucky? He called me sir." Wilbur shook hands with him. "And look at that. He's shaking hands with me. Twenty years on the force and it finally happened. Now, this kid I like. I don't think I've seen you around here, Gustave."

"You can call him Gus," I offered, as I sipped from my coffee cup. Crenshaw regarded me with a sneer before turning back to his new plaything.

"Where are you from, Gustave?"

"I'm from Minnesota, sir. The St. Cloud area," said Gus.

"Are you now? What happened to your face, Gustave? Looks like you got kicked by a Holstein."

"Gus is a boxer," I blurted.

"Is that so?"

"Yes, sir."

"Yeah, I can see that. Big farm kid like you. You're pig-lifting strong, aren't you? You got yourself some meaty hands too. Firm grip when you shake hands. I also noticed your hands are all scrapped-up on the knuckles, Gustave. Do you wear boxing gloves during your bouts in Minnesota? Or do you bare-knuckle it?"

"I wear gloves, sir," said Gus, as he eased his hands under the table.

But it was too late. Crenshaw had already taken inventory. I told you he was sharp. He notices everything.

"I also see some flecks of blood on your jacket sleeves—down by the buttons. And you got a nasty tear there in the shoulder. You box with your jacket on, Gustave?"

"No, sir."

"Yes, sir, no, sir. I don't think this city has seen the likes of you in a while, boy. So tell me, how'd you get blood on yourself?"

"He got mugged," I interjected.

"Mugged, you say? Did you report it to the police, Gustave?"

"Why bother doing that?" I snorted. "A thousand people a day get mugged in this city. I don't recall ever seeing a single mugger being arrested."

"Is that a slam against the force, Bucky? Because if it is, I—"

"What do you want, Wilbur? Is there a reason you're harassing us?"

Crenshaw swung around to face me. His eyes drilled into mine, but he spoke to Gus. "How long have you known this guy, Gustave?"

Gus hesitated. "Just since last night, sir."

Wilbur's left eye squinted suspiciously at that news. "Last night, uh? New friends. Aw, that's sweet. What do you know about your new friend, Gustave?"

His stare down with me continued.

"Uh...I know his name is Buck. I don't recall his last name."

A sour grin slithered across Crenshaw's face. "Yeah, but do you know who he really is? What he does for a living?"

"No, sir. He never said."

"Well Gustave, this new friend of yours is a—"

"Gus, why don't you switch tables for a minute while the detective and I talk," I blurted.

"Naw, Gustave, you stay right there," said Crenshaw, patting Gus's shoulder. "You might learn some things about the kind of company you keep in the big city. I wouldn't want a nice kid like you getting all polluted."

Gus gave me a quizzical look.

"Why are you here, Wilbur?" I asked, pushing my plate aside.

He leaned in, his eyes scouring my face. "Where were you last night, Bucky?"

"I was at the Famous Door, it's a jazz club down on—"

"Yeah, yeah, I know the place. Who was playing last night?"

"Bob Howard. He plays the piano. Do you know what a piano is?"

His lip curled. "What time were you there?"

"From nine o'clock until almost midnight. You can ask Socks, the door-man down there. He can vouch for me." Everyone knows Socks. I was sure that Wilbur knew him, too.

"Midnight, huh? How about after that?"

"I was home."

"All night?"

"Ask Gus, he was there."

Crenshaw raised an eyebrow. A smirk formed. He glanced at Gus and back. "You boys have a sleepover? I thought you liked girls, Bucky. I guess I was wrong."

Gus cocked his head as if he didn't quite understand the implication.

"Look, Wilbur," I said, "I was coming home from The Famous Door when I ran into Gus here. He appeared to be lost. He had been mugged. I felt sorry for him, so I gave him a bite to eat and he slept on my couch—saved him the price of a hotel."

"That's pretty generous of you, Bucky." He leaned back, drumming his fingers on the table's edge. "How about Union Square?"

"What about it?"

"Were you anywhere in the vicinity?"

I had a feeling it was coming, so I didn't allow my face to react. "Sure. I've been to Union Square plenty of times. They have a statue of Lafayette there. I waved to him a couple of weeks ago. He didn't wave back."

"How about last night?"

"What about last night?"

"Were you down by Union Square?"

"How could I've been there last night? I already told you where I was. Ask Gus, he'll tell ya." I figured my best chance of getting out of being grilled was to have choir-boy vouch for me.

Crenshaw shot Gus a glance.

Gus nodded. "It's just like he says, sir. We met on the street and then we went to his place. He gave me bologna sandwiches."

"Bologna, huh? Sounds delicious. You were there all night?"

"That's right, sir."

"Did Bucky leave for any reason during the night?"

"No, sir. We talked a while and then we both went to bed." Gus's eyes went big for a second before blurting, "Uh, that is, I slept on the couch in his living room, and he slept...you know...in his room."

Crenshaw leaned toward him as if attempting to suck truth from his skin. He stared at Gus with his beady little eyes. Gus stayed stock still, looking right back at him. Corn-fed honesty versus New York shrewdness. Corn-fed won. The detective relaxed and sat back in the booth. His fingers continued to drum.

"What's this all about, Wilbur?" I asked innocently.

He worked his mouth around, his lips doing the hula. "We found an open safe this morning in an office building down off of Union Square. It was empty. Thought maybe it had some help getting open—and getting empty."

I held my face straight, but cringed inside. I'd made a stupid mistake. I had forgotten to close the safe before leaving. But then tripping over a dead body has a way of knocking incidentals off the old thinking block.

"Why come to me about that?"

"Don't act all innocent with me, Bucky. I know what you're capable of. I find an open, empty safe and a few select characters jump into my brain box—your name is at the top of the list."

I could feel Gus giving me a curious look as I held Crenshaw's stare.

Sometimes the truth is the best policy, so that's what I gave him: "I swear to you on my life, Wilbur, that I did not crack any safe last night." Leaving out, of course, the part about the safe already being open.

Detective Crenshaw simmered. His eyes were suspicious beads. He glanced back at Gus. "And you can alibi him for the night? All night?"

"Yes, sir."

He slanted a look back at me. His mouth twitched like he didn't fully believe it, but he finally crawled out of the booth and stood. Hitched up his trousers. Bumped the brim of his fedora up. Didn't take his eyes off me.

"You better be leveling with me, Bucky. I'd hate to be arresting you for..."

He stopped himself.

He'd almost slipped and said, 'murder', but he hadn't mentioned that crime yet. He was playing it close to the vest. And I wasn't about to probe him about it further. As he had one foot out the door, I didn't want him lingering any longer than necessary.

"I'll keep my ears open, Detective," I said. "If I hear anything on the street that can help with your investigation, I'll be sure to call you right away."

He grunted. "Don't get syrupy with me, Bucky." He slid a look toward Gus. "How long you in town for, hayseed?"

"Until I'm not, sir," said Gus.

Good answer. I smiled.

Crenshaw flicked a nod my way. "If I were you, I would steer clear of this one, or he'll be dragging you into his criminal ways."

"Hey," I said. "Don't be slandering my good name to my friends."

Crenshaw planted his mitts on the table's edge and leaned in close enough to lick my nose. "You're a thief, Flynn. A lousy thief."

I resented that. I'm not a lousy thief, I'm a talented thief. And having never been caught proves it. But to him I said: "Where's your proof, Wilbur?"

He hovered, steaming.

"Have I ever been arrested?"

"You've been brought in for questioning."

"Ever charged?"

"Not yet."

"Have I ever spent one night in jail?"

"Not that I know of."

"I've never even been given a ticket for loitering or jaywalking. Yet you're always calling me a criminal. I'm feeling a little hurt by that."

"Are you now? I'm so sorry. I would hate to bruise your dandelion feelings." He pushed off the table to stand at full height, all five-foot-six of it. "Don't disappear on me, Flynn. I may want to talk to you about this some more."

"You know where to find me."

"Yeah, I do." He turned and stomped out of the diner. He didn't even pause to give Rosy Grace a second consideration.

13

My eyes remained on Wilbur as he stomped down the sidewalk. Remaining quiet, I raised my hand to hush Gus when he attempted to ask a question. I waited until Wilbur got to his cruiser. He turned, and I gave a light-hearted wave. He scowled, got in, and slammed the door shut. Once he pulled away from the curb. I turned to Gus.

"We need to get you someplace fast, so you can hide out for a while."

"Hide out? What are you talking about?"

"So far, it looks like you're safe. Crenshaw doesn't know you're involved. He hasn't placed you at the scene yet, but it's only a matter of time."

"Involved in what? What scene are you talking about?"

"Manny Greenstreet's office."

"What about it?"

"Crenshaw was just asking about the safe in Greenstreet's office."

"How do you know that? He didn't mention Mr. Greenstreet. Say, what was all that stuff about you being a thief?"

"We'll talk about that later. For now, we just need to get you on the down and low for a few hours before Wilbur discovers you were at Greenstreet's last night."

"But I was there last night."

"That's right. And there were witnesses, too. Witnesses that could testify to what you did."

"You mean throwing the desk around?"

"Yeah," I said cautiously. "Throwing the desk around."

"Look, if Mr. Greenstreet wants to charge me for damages, I'll pay him back. I'll even wrestle for him if I have to. No need to drag the police into it."

"You won't be paying Greenstreet back for anything, Gus. He's dead."

Gus's jaw dropped. "Dead? Mr. Greenstreet is dead? What are you talking about?"

"Someone murdered him last night."

Shear wonderment slapped him across the face. I didn't need to ask if he'd killed Greenstreet or not. His corn-fed expression said it all. This kid had to be innocent. Had to be.

"How...how do you know that?"

"We'll talk about that later, too. First things first. We need to hide you out for a while."

I stood. Gus did too, a bit mystified. He started to ask another question, but I shushed him. I was trying to think of where to go. My apartment was out. Once Crenshaw discovered that Gus was at the wrestling club last night, that would be the first place he'd look.

Behind the diner's countertop was a pass-through window into the kitchen. Steam vapors of sizzling bacon and sausage swirled. I could see Whitey talking with the fry cook. If I were to ask him for a favor, he would let us hang out at his place for the day, but his wife would be there too, and I did not want to drag either of them into it. It would be just like Wilbur to try and charge them with harboring a murder suspect.

Trudy lingered behind the counter, leaning back with a cigarette between her pink lips. She watched us with crossed arms. We had hardly touched our breakfasts. I could see questions curling up into her dinner plate face.

Then it came to me! The most obvious answer of all—Nick Terrano. Nick was one of Pops' closest friends. He owns Terrano's Gym down on W. 28th Street. He's a fight trainer. He would let Gus hang out in his gym in a heartbeat.

"Leaving so soon?" came Trudy's voice from behind the counter. "You haven't even finished your—" She shot a wrathful glance toward the crowd at the other end of the dinner, which ricocheted back to me with a glare of fury. "Hey! Don't you even think of moving down to those tables, Buck Flynn!"

I quickly pulled some bills out of my wallet and threw them on the table—more than enough to cover the meal and her tip. I then raised my hands in surrender. "We're not moving, Trudy, we're done with breakfast."

She was suddenly at the table, scooping up the money. "The cop scare you off, honey?" she asked with a giggle.

I squinted at her. "You didn't call to let him know I was here, did you?"

Her round face fell with shock, her enormous lashes batted as she blinked. She genuinely looked hurt.

"I would never do that!" She croaked. "You're one of my favorite customers, Buck."

In my peripheral vision, I caught the form of Rosy Grace reaching for a ticket on the menu carousel in the window to the kitchen. The men behind her were craning their necks, appreciating the reach.

"I might be your only customer, Trudy."

"I'm no rat-fink," she muttered. "I would never call the cops on someone and I should clobber you for thinking so."

I knew she could do it, so I gave her a quick peck on the cheek and backed away.

"Come on, Gus," I said. "Let's go before Wilbur comes back."

———◇———

We took a cab, even though the gym is just a few blocks away and we could've walked it. But I wanted to make sure we weren't being followed by Wilbur or any of his cop-cronies. I had the cabbie do a few curly-ques through Manhattan before dropping us off a block away.

As we walked down the street toward Nick's place, Gus said, "I don't understand. Why do I have to hide from the police? I'm willing to tell them what happened. And I still don't get how you know that Mr. Greenstreet is dead. The police officer never mentioned it."

I decided to give it to him straight. I stopped in the middle of the sidewalk and faced him, grabbing him by arms.

"Listen, Gus, Greenstreet got his noggin bashed in last night. Someone killed him with a leg from the desk you busted up."

Gus blinked. "How on earth do you know that?"

"Look, I was there, okay?"

"Where?"

"Greenstreet's office."

"When?"

"Last night."

"You were there when Mr. Greenstreet was killed?"

"No. I got there...after."

"But..."

"Look, I went down to the wrestling club last night after you conked out on the couch. I wanted to help you out. I thought maybe I could get that contract back."

"My contract? How? Did you talk to Mr. Greenstreet about it?"

"No. I just told you, he was dead already."

"Dead...?" He looked numb. "But you thought maybe he would give the contract to you?"

"No. I had something else in mind."

"Like what?"

"Like taking it from Manny's safe without him knowing."

"From Mr. Greenstreet's safe?" He gasped, literally an open-mouth gasp. "Then...you are a thief."

The poor kid had the look of someone whose favorite politician had just been brought up on corruption charges.

"So you lied to the police officer. You did crack open his safe."

"No. I didn't...exactly. Someone got there first. The safe was already unlocked—and picked clean. That's when I saw the body."

"You saw Mr. Greenstreet dead?"

I nodded.

"But...you didn't..." Panic flashed in his eyes. "It wasn't you?"

The look in his eyes had the same wariness that I had about him earlier this morning. Now it was him wondering if he was looking at a killer.

"Of course not, Gus. I'm not a killer. Sure, I've broken into a safe here and there, but I've never killed anyone."

He stared at me, wavering, and wondering if he could trust me. It hurt me a little.

"Listen, the reason we need to get you off the street is that your fingerprints are probably all over the murder weapon, and in the office. Someone bashed in his head with a leg you broke off of the desk. And once Crenshaw asks around, he's going to find out that some Swedish guy from Michigan—"

"Minnesota."

"Minnesota...was there throwing a tantrum. He'll arrest you for sure."

"But I didn't do it."

"You know that...and I know that, but Crenshaw will want to peg you for it."

"You think he'll arrest me?"

"Of course he'll arrest you. And me too, just for feeding you bologna sandwiches."

"And for breaking into the safe."

"I'm telling you I didn't break..."

The lunkhead was smiling back at me.

"You're pulling my chain, Swede."

"You don't think I killed Mr. Greenstreet, do you?"

I hesitated. "No. I don't. Maybe I did a little, at first. But not now."

"I don't think you did it either, Buck," he said, giving me a playful punch to the shoulder. I managed to stay upright, but I'm not gonna lie. It hurt a little.

"Great," I replied. "We're both innocent of murder. We can break out the Champaign and toast the fact later. Now let's get you off the street."

14

I led him into Terrano's Gym. We walked across the lobby to a wide staircase leading up to the second floor to where the gym is located.

Climbing the stairs, we were met with gymnasium smells, sweat, muscle balm, talcum powder. Gym sounds were there too. Grunts. Huffs. Gloves smacking flesh. Trainers yelling. As we reached the second floor, we found the double doors to the gym were open for added ventilation. A dozen or so men were inside. Some running laps around the perimeter, some lifting iron, some punching speed bags. A couple of men were in the ring in the center of the floor, sparring. They both wore protective headgear.

I spotted Nick on the floor next to the ring, leaning on the ropes as he watched the two guys go at it.

"Footwork, Murphy!" Nick was yelling. "Move the feet. You're standing there waiting for him to come at ya, you stupid Mick."

"Hey Nick," I said, as we drew up next to him.

Nick glanced my way. "Well, look what the cat dragged in. Buck Flynn. What are you doing here?"

He gave me a friendly punch in the arm, but I'd braced myself for it and didn't go flying into next Tuesday. Between him and Gus, I'd probably be black and blue tomorrow.

Twenty-five years ago, Nick Terrano was a welterweight champion, known for his speed, his effortless footwork, and a hammering right-handed uppercut. Even today heavyweight contenders, twice his size, tremble in his presence and listen attentively to his professional advice.

At first glance, Nick doesn't look like a former boxer. He's not tall or full of balloon muscles. At five foot nine, he's quite slender, with slightly hunched shoulders. But a second look tells a different story. Beneath his short-sleeved, collared shirt are corded muscles, streamlined, like a jaguar. And the way he carries himself gives the impression of being tightly coiled, ready to explode. His movements are fluid, effortless, yet determined and quick, as if unpredictable. He has dark, sad-sack eyes set in puffy pockets the color of avocado skin, and his glare is penetrating, as if constantly sizing you up, looking for your weaknesses and vulnerabilities—even now during a friendly chat.

"What brings you here, Buck?" He glanced over at Gus. "And who's this character?"

Gus offered his hand. "Gustave Nordstrom, sir," he said.

Nick's eyes widened. "Sir? Don't call me that, I'm just as good as you."

Gus blinked, the old army joke going over his head.

Nick shook his hand. "Looks like you've been in a fight, son," said Nick.

Gus shrugged. "Kind of."

"You're supposed to duck when fists come your way. Don't be like Murphy here." He chucked his thumb toward the ring. "He just stands there and takes it."

Gus grinned. "There were just too many fists coming at me to avoid, sir."

"Gus got pounced on by five professional wrestlers," I said.

Nick raised his eyebrows. "Five, you say. What do they look like?"

"I did some damage," said Gus proudly.

"I bet you did."

"Look, Nick," I interjected. "Could I talk to you privately for a minute?"

"Sure, Buck. We can go back to the office." He swung another look at the sparring taking place in the ring. "Feet, Murphy! Move your feet," he yelled. He shook his head as he looked back at me. "Dumb mick. He thinks it's all about fists and right hooks. Doesn't even know that God grew feet at the end of his sticks."

I turned to Gus to inform him I wanted to talk to Nick alone for a few minutes, but he had already moved over to ringside to watch the boxers. His face scrunched in concentration, evaluating.

"That's a good-sized boy," said Nick. "He's a fighter, I can tell. The way he carries himself. And just look at him, staring at those guys in the ring. He's studying them."

"Nick, that's exactly what I want to talk to you about."

Nick and I walked across the gym to his office at the far end. His door has a frosted glass window with block lettering that reads: *Nick Terrano, Proprietor and Manager.* As a joke, someone had hand-painted below it *and one mean SOB.* Nick apparently took the insult as a compliment and never had it removed. Next to the door was a handwritten poster from Nick himself, offering pertinent advice for those coming inside: *No bleeding in my office...no crying either.*

We entered, and Nick took a seat behind his desk. I grabbed one of the two wooden chairs that he keeps for company.

"You in trouble, Buck?" He asked, as he swung his legs up on top of his desk and leaned back in his chair.

That's the way it is with Nick. He goes straight to the issue. No beating around the bush. It was the same way he fought years ago. The minute the bell rang, it was go time.

"Not yet," I said, "but I've got Wilbur Crenshaw breathing on my neck."

"Crenshaw? What's he after this time?"

"Nothing that I can't handle for myself, but my chief concern is for Gus."

Nick eyed me. "Does it have anything to do with him being pounced on by five wrestlers?"

"Some. How much do you know of the wrestling game here in town?"

"Not much. I know it's all for show—all prance and dance. A bunch of big guys dress up in costumes and play-act in front of big crowds."

"You think it's all fake?"

"Sure, it's fake. It's a show. Like a play. Don't get me wrong, the guys in the ring are athletes—and they have to know their stuff, otherwise, they'll get hurt for real—but don't be betting on the wrestling game. It's all programmed."

"Ever hear of a guy named Manny Greenstreet?"

Nick grunted. "You mean Manford Greenstreet, the greasy little weasel who has a two-bit outfit over by Union Square?"

"That's the guy."

Concern creased his brow. "If your boy out there wants to get into the wrestling game, you—"

"He's not," I blurted. "But he's got himself entangled in a bit of a jam. He was misled."

"By Greenstreet?"

I nodded.

"Your buddy needs to steer clear of Manny. He'll get soaked. The guy's no good."

"Well, steering clear of Greenstreet won't be too much of a problem now. Manny got his ticket punched last night."

Nick sat up, his legs came down. "No kidding. Manny Greenstreet? How?"

"Someone bashed his head in."

Nick cocked his head. "Your big friend out there?"

"Naw. At least I don't think so. But it looks bad for him."

I filled Nick in on the situation. I told him everything, including how I dropped in to check out Manny Greenstreet's safe and found him bludgeoned to death. Nick knows how I make a living. He knew Pops' way of life too. They were friends as kids. He and Pops even collaborated on a couple of jobs together back in the day. Their paths took different directions, but they remained friends. A few times, when lines needed to be crossed, Pops helped him out. Don't ask me how. They never told me. Boxing isn't the cleanest sport in New York, and a few unpleasant characters lurk in the shadows.

For the most part, Nick's on the up and up, but over the years he's had to put the hurt on a few cheap hoods who had tried to push him around. You would think that being Italian, Nick might be connected. But as far as I know, he's not. Sure, he knows guys, but who doesn't.

In the early years, after Pops got plugged, I spent many a night sleeping in this very office. I also trained with Nick some, when no one else was around. He showed me a few street moves that would be illegal in the ring—mostly for defense. But he never let me take up boxing as a sport. Pops wouldn't allow it, and Nick honored that. Pops told me it could ruin my hands for box work. It's hard to spin the dials (or pick pockets, for that matter) when your fingers are as dead as sausage links. Besides, I'm not built for boxing—climbing rooftops and scaling walls with ropes, yes—boxing, no.

Nick took my tale in stride. Nodding at some parts, raising an eyebrow at others. He perked up when I told him about Gus being undefeated in the mid-west.

"Wait, he's not the guy they call, *The Storming Swede*, is he?" He asked.

"One and the same."

"A guy from Chi-town told me about him. Has a vicious right hook from what I hear. Be a shame to have him wearing leotards in some sham-show."

When I got to the part about finding Manny Greenstreet with his brains bashed in, Nick grew somber. "And you're sure the kid didn't do it?"

I shook my head. "I don't think so. I hope he didn't. Besides, I don't think he would use a piece of wood when his fists could do it just as good."

"And what do you think happened to his contract with Manny?"

"That's what I'm going to try and find out. What do you know of Greenstreet's partner...some guy named Jacobs?"

"That would be Mickey Jacobs. Used to be a fighter himself years ago. Could've been a good heavyweight, but he had no self-control in the ring. His temper always got the better of him."

"Temper you say?" I liked the sound of that. Anything to take the focus away from Gus.

"Yeah. Hot-heads make for poor fighters. They get all hopped up on fury and lose sight of the goal. Those angry guys come out strong at the opening bell—full of bluster and arm swinging—but they rarely have anything left in the tank by the fourth round. They don't know how to box smart."

"When did he switch to wrestling?"

"Can't say for sure, but I know that after his career was over he settled for being a manager for wrestlers, and when he first started recruiting wrestlers he tried passing himself off as Mike Jacobs for a while."

The name jolted me. "Aha, Mike Jacobs, the famous fight promoter here in town. That's why the name Mickey Jacobs sounded familiar when Gus mentioned it earlier."

"Yeah, but don't get the two mixed up. Mickey started telling the kids he was trying to recruit that he was, the Mike Jacobs, to get them to sign, but when the real Mr. Jacobs heard about it he had to send some guys over to give him a talking to. He became just Mickey after that."

I could only imagine the kind of 'talking to' he got.

"Is the guy dangerous?" I asked.

Nick went quiet for a minute. Then he said. "I think he can be...if he gets cornered."

"Do you have an address for him, besides the gym off of Union Square?"

"Maybe." He reached over and pulled a Rolodex across the desk and flipped through it. "Yeah, here he is."

He gave me the address, writing it down on a piece of paper. I tucked it into my wallet.

"Better be careful around that one, Buck. Don't get caught alone with him. Anything I taught you, he knows in spades. He packed a mean punch in his day. I don't want you getting hurt."

"Do you happen to know the name of Manny Greenstreet's lawyer?"

"Nope. But I can ask around if you like. What do you want with him?"

"According to Gus, Greenstreet's lawyer has been out of town for a few days—that's why Manny still had the contract. Gus said that Manny had planned on running it up to his lawyer first thing this morning. He never got the chance. The contract has disappeared from the safe—and Manny ain't running nowhere now."

"So if the lawyer hasn't got the contract, what do you want with him?"

I shrugged. "You never know. It might have found its way to him somehow. If nothing else pans out, I figure a nighttime visit to his office wouldn't hurt—just to make sure."

"I'll put some calls in, see what I can find out. How will I get a hold of you?"

I paused, thinking. The problem is, I don't have a phone in my apartment. We have a house phone for the building mounted on the wall on the second floor, but Mr. Gunderson, the old coot with the apartment closest to it, is always the first to answer it and is rarely willing to walk up the two flights to let me know that I have a call coming in. He just ends up hanging up on the caller.

"I'll give you a call later this afternoon before you leave the gym," I said, "And if I miss you here, I'll call you at home."

Nick frowned. "If my wife answers, hang up. If she knows it's you, she'll just be trying to fix you up with Franny or Gina again."

Francesca and Regina are his daughters, and Nick's Italian wife, Angelica, has been trying for years to match me up with one of them. However, there are a couple of problems with that.

For one thing, the girls are just plain gruesome to behold. Looking at Nick—who is somewhat gruesome himself—you would tend to blame the faulty genes on him, but truth be told, the girls take after their mother. I won't say anything more about that.

The second thing is that Nick's wife, Angelica, does *not* know what I do for a living—being a thief and all. Nick, however, does. And he doesn't want his daughters getting mixed up with a criminal. I can't blame him. The guy only wants best for his girls. If I had a daughter, I wouldn't want her dating the likes of me, either.

So, as hard as Angelica works to snare me for one of them, Nick works just as hard to keep me away. I suppose his reticence should offend me, but truthfully, I'm just glad that he's not pushing one of them on me as well. Nick thinks his girls are the most beautiful creatures on God's green earth, and I don't have the heart to tell him otherwise.

"So Nick," I said. "You care if Gus hangs out here for a day or two—until I get this taken care of?"

"Is the heat after him?"

"I won't lie to you, Nick. I already told you that Wilbur Crenshaw is working the case. He hasn't put Gus at the scene yet, but he will."

"And you don't think he did Manny in?"

I did my best to sound believable. "No. Not at all!"

Nick rubbed his chin as he contemplated the implications of it. No one likes it when trouble gets dumped on their doorstep, and it was a big favor to ask; but I was hoping our relationship—and his relationship with my Pops as well—would count for something.

He leaned forward and was about to speak when the office door burst open. A trainer jammed his head in, all excited.

"Sorry to bust in like this, Nick," he spouted in a flurry of words. "But you gotta see this. Some guy in street clothes just put Murphy down on the canvas."

—◆—

15

NICK WAS OUT OF his seat and through the door in a blink. I followed. We rushed into the gym and up to the ring.

A small crowd of men had gathered on the floor there, staring through the ropes. A couple of guys were in the ring, kneeling over a boxer, the one called Murphy. He was sitting upright on the canvas, but droopy, and obviously shaken. His head was waddling, as if trying to shake the stars away.

That's when I noticed that one of the guys in the ring was Gus. He was bracing the guy up, trying to console him—or revive him. It took me a second to register that Gus had his jacket off and was wearing boxing gloves.

"What's going on?" yelled Nick

"Some kid took Murph out," said someone standing on the floor.

"Got him with a right hook," said another.

"You should'a heard it. POW."

"He's alright," said the other man kneeling on the canvas next to Gus. "Just got his bell rung."

Gus and the other man helped the dazed boxer to his feet and walked him to the corner. Someone slipped a stool through the ropes and they gently eased Murphy down onto it. Another man suddenly appeared and climbed into the ring. He carried a medical bag. He studied the boxer, lifting his chin to look into his eyes with a retinoscope.

Murphy angrily slapped the equipment away. "I'm okay...leave me alone," he snarled. "Stupid kid sucker punched me."

Gus looked over at us, embarrassed. "I'm sorry, Mr. Terrano. I didn't mean to hurt him. We were just sparring."

Nick hesitated when he spotted Gus in his street clothes. "Who let you in the ring dressed like that?"

"Murphy did, sir," said one of the other fighters.

"Murph was taunting him, Nick," said the trainer who had come to get us. "The kid was offering some advice, but Murph wasn't taking it."

"I was only trying to help him with his footwork," said Gus. "Just like you were...but..."

"Murph got snappy with the kid," said one of the other guys standing there. "Challenged him to climb in and show him how it was done. I think Murph intended to teach the kid a lesson."

"Only the kid had moves," said the trainer. "Started dancing, shuffling easy like, trying to get Murph to follow."

"The kid was looking down at his feet, demonstrating, when Murph blindsided him with a cross," interjected someone.

"So it was Murph who threw the sucker punch?" asked Nick.

"Yeah, that's right. But it never connected."

"I have never seen such a quick block," said one man.

"Lightning in a bottle," said the trainer. "That's when the kid threw the right hook."

"Just one."

"Pure instinct."

"Murph had no time to dodge."

"The stupid mick doesn't move," muttered Nick.

Murphy, still on his stool and still loopy, turned his head to glare at Nick.

Gus came to ropes, his face scrunched with concern. "I'm awful sorry, Mr. Terrano. Mr. Murphy claimed to be a professional fighter. I thought he was."

"Yeah," mumbled Nick, "I thought so too."

Nick swung around to face me. For a second, I thought he was about to chew my face off.

"Yeah, the kid can hang around for a while," he said.

Gus, Nick, and I went back into Nick's office, where Nick grilled him about his career in Minnesota. Gus was modest about it at first and seemed embarrassed about mentioning his undefeated record.

"My folks taught me not to boast," he offered.

But Nick was curious and began throwing out names of fighters he knew from the mid-west. Gus opened up. "Oh sure, I know him," he said, "I beat him in Minneapolis one night," or "Klanski? The guy has a glass jaw. I put him down in the first round."

Nick was impressed.

As I left, the two of them were still yakking and laughing, getting along as if they'd always known each other. The last thing I heard as I was leaving the office was Nick saying, "Come to my house for dinner tonight, Gus, I want you to meet my wife and daughters."

Uh-oh. Fresh meat for the hounds.

At least he's not a thief.

16

HAVING SLEPT VERY LITTLE last night, I was dead on my feet and my head was filling with bricks. I could've used a nap, but going back to my apartment was not an option. With Detective Crenshaw investigating Manny Greenstreet's murder, it wouldn't be long before he placed Gus at the crime scene. Then, putting two and two together, he would realize that the thief he'd questioned this morning at Whitey's had been hanging out with a prime suspect for murder. He wouldn't be happy and my place would be his first stop.

Gus, of course, would be his primary target, but no doubt he'd be after me, too. The circumstantial evidence did not favor us: a sleaze-bag promoter is murdered in a room with an opened safe, and the two guys who just happen to be eating breakfast together, are a known thief and a temper-throwing Swede with a pretty good motive for wanting to have the said sleaze-bag out of his life. Looking through his cop-lens, Crenshaw was sure to assume the two of us were guilty of all sorts of mayhem. And because I hadn't been forthright with him this morning, it only compounded the illusion of guilt.

While Crenshaw has always been a thorn in my side, I've been his thorn, too. Over the years, he's never been able to nab me for anything, and it has frustrated him to no end. I suppose, in one sense, I'm his great white whale. And if he could wrap me up for murder, it would be his crowning achievement as a cop. A feat he would relish.

Don't get me wrong, Crenshaw isn't the type to plant evidence; mostly, he's an honest cop, but me being within proximity of a murder suspect—like feeding him bologna sandwiches—was enough to bring up some kind of charges. Anything to get me behind bars.

Leaving that safe door open had been a stupid mistake. Pops would not be proud. It had brought the heat down on my head. But compounding that mistake was the haunting possibility that I could have left trace evidence behind in Manny's office. I didn't think I had, but who knows?

All that aside, what concerned me the most was Crenshaw becoming so focused on the two of us that he could overlook evidence pointing to Greenstreet's actual killer. Cops can get myopic. Once they set their sights on a suspect (or in this case, suspects), they get closed off to other possibilities. Cops love closing cases. The hell with truth and justice. We found the killer(s)...let 'em swing!

Gus and I could both be in jail by nightfall.

Maybe. But just maybe I could do something about it. As sleep wasn't an option, I decided to hop down to Union Square, swing by the wrestling club, and watch the situation for a while. See if something turned up. Yes, it would be risky getting close to the situation that way—I certainly didn't want to accidentally run into Crenshaw—but what choice did I have?

I grabbed a cab to E. 17th Street, got out, and walked across the Square toward 14th Street. The place was jumping at this time of day—nothing like the deadness of last night. Automobiles, taxis, and buses clogged the streets. The sidewalks were thick with people. S. Klein's was open, of course, shoppers streaming in and out. Across the face of the building were signs advertising dresses, coats, suits, and millinery.

I circled around the statue of Lafayette. He hadn't moved a muscle since last night. His left hand was still looking for alms. I paused beneath his pedestal of Quincy quartz, and a thought struck me.

Simply hanging around outside the Knickerbocker Wrestling Federation would be pretty foolish—too much exposure. If Crenshaw spotted me, he'd be suspicious, and if nothing else, he might lock me up on a frivolous charge, expecting me to spill the beans about where Gus was holed up—which would be a long wait on his part. Besides, loitering near a murder scene could arouse the curiosity of any random cop, even if it wasn't Crenshaw.

So what should I do?

Then an idea came to me.

I glanced around, taking in the variety of storefronts that made up Union Square. I immediately landed on one that fit my needs perfectly.

A hardware store.

I headed that way, knowing that I needed to make a quick purchase before going over to the wrestling club.

Inside the store, I grabbed a cheap pair of pliers, a roll of electrical tape, and a small packet of 16 gauge copper wire. I paid for the items and, once outside, I found an empty bench next to my friend Lafayette where I could sit and do a bit of arts and crafts.

The idea I had would keep me out of sight and provide the perfect vantage point from which to observe the club. It had to do with that abandoned building across the street, the one whose doorway I had hidden in last night before entering the club. The windows were boarded up, and the door padlocked. If I remembered right, the building was three stories tall, and I figured the roof would give me a bird's-eye view of the action below.

The only hitch was the padlock on the door. Unfortunately, I had left the apartment this morning without my caddy of lock-picks, having stowed them away in the air shaft.

Which meant I had to improvise.

Using the pliers, I twisted off a couple of lengths of wire and then bent the ends into a couple of makeshift lock-picks. They weren't perfect—nothing like the set Pops had made for me—but they would do.

Opening up the packet of electrical tape, I wrapped the other ends with enough tape to create small handles on each pick, giving me something to grip other than the slick wire. I pocketed the hardware items—just in case I needed to make adjustments in the field—and then slipped both lock-picks into the breast pocket of my jacket.

I headed out.

I stopped at a street vendor along the way and bought a bag of roasted peanuts. Detective Crenshaw had interrupted our breakfast this morning, and I was growing hungry. I tucked the bag into the pocket with the pliers and continued towards 14th Street.

I turned down the block to where the Knickerbocker Wrestling Federation was situated. Staying on the opposite side of the street, I approached the abandoned building. I scanned the scene across the way, watching for cops.

Two police cruisers were parked outside, but they were empty. A saw-horse barricade blocked off the entrance to the building. The coroner's wagon must have come and gone because I didn't see it anywhere. Manny Greenstreet was probably already downtown, laid out on a slab. Thankfully, no cops lingered outside, and there was no sign of Sergeant Detective Wilbur Crenshaw.

I needed to get off the street as quickly as possible.

I leaped up the stoop of the abandoned building, withdrawing my makeshift lock-picks as I did so. Thankfully, the door recessed back from the stoop by a couple of feet. It gave me some cover.

Crouching in front of the door, I looked the lock over. It connected a chain looped through the handles on a set of double doors. It was an older brass Slaymaker padlock. Pops had at least ten of these lying around the house years ago, and I had one or two in my collection on the wall of my apartment. I had hours of practice on them, but that had been with actual lock-picks, not wire.

Oh well. Make do.

I stuck the 16 gauge wire into the slot and fiddled about. I had kept the pliers in case I needed to make adjustments to the ends. I felt exposed. Cops were just across the street. If one was watching from a window, he might wonder what I was up to and come sniffing around.

It took longer than normal, at least sixty seconds longer—which can feel like an eternity when exposed that way—but thankfully I didn't need to make adjustments to the picks and the lock finally fell open. I unraveled the chain from the door handles, hooked the opened lock through one of the chain links, and gave a tug on a door. The ancient hinges creaked loud enough to send chills down my spine. But the door opened, and I quickly slipped inside.

———◆———

17

THE PLACE SMELLED LIKE dust, but it wasn't as dark as I had expected. Four large windows ran across the face of the building, two on either side of the door, and although planks boarded up the window outside, streaks of sunlight filtered through the cracks, creating a subtle sepia glow inside.

Tables and chairs sat stacked to the left. Straight ahead, a waist-high counter sat a few feet from the back wall, a menu placard behind it. Genius thief that I am, I quickly ascertained that the place had once been a restaurant.

Against the right-hand wall, a narrow set of stairs led to the upper stories. However, the steps looked iffy. Caked with dry-rot, a few of the runners were missing. The banister, too, hung loose and busted, as if ready to topple. I shuddered at the thought of climbing a pile of rotting wood. If I crashed through from an upper story landing and broke a leg, it could be months before they found me.

So far, my plan of establishing a rooftop crow's nest wasn't panning out.

Turning back to the front windows, I stepped over to the nearest one and found I could peer between the slats to get a narrow view of the wrestling club across the way. Checking the other windows, I realized each window offered a variety of cracks and angles.

I wouldn't be needing the stairs after all. It might not be a bird's-eye view, but I was happy to settle for a peek-a-boo view.

I pulled out a chair from the stack to the left, dusted it off with my handkerchief, and placed it in front of the widest crack I could find. Reaching into my pocket, I withdrew my bag of peanuts and began enjoying the show.

It made for pretty boring entertainment.

Once in a while, a cop moseyed outside to check for something in one of the cruisers, or to smoke a cigarette, but that was about all.

A few civilians drifted in and out of the front doors, both men and women, professionally dressed in suits and dresses, all of whom had the stricken look that comes from being in the vicinity of violence. I realized that parts of the building on the upper floors possibly contained professional offices, so these people most likely had nothing to do with the Knickerbocker Wrestling Federation at all. None of them looked suspicious, just green around the gills, and I didn't spot anyone who stood out as being a wrestler.

Plenty of pedestrians passed by from both directions. Most perked up as they approached the obvious police presence—curiosity seekers—gawking at the club's front doors, maybe hoping for a glimpse at whatever juicy excitement was happening inside. However, they quickly moved on when they realized that there was nothing to report.

I sat there for nearly an hour, slowly whittling away at my bag of peanuts. Boredom set in, as well as a growing frustration that I wasn't accomplishing anything by sitting here. Watching the club was not helping Gus's situation at all.

A tall, striking woman with black hair wearing a blue dress came out of the front doors. Even from across the street, I could tell she was a looker. Her hips swayed elegantly as she maneuvered around the saw-horse barriers. Sashaying down the street, she cast a glance back toward the building she had just left, and a smile crested her face, a pretty, confident smile that told the world she would not let a little murder in the building ruin her day. I liked her for it. It even brought a smile to my face.

Finishing the last of my peanuts, I was crumpling the bag to toss aside when a man leaped up the stoop just outside my abandoned building, startling me. I jumped from my chair, nearly knocking it over.

Was he coming into the building? Had someone called about an intruder?

Panic flooded me.

With my eyes drilled on the door, I quickly backed away, wondering where I could hide if it suddenly flung open. The only place available was the counter near the back wall. Not the best place. If someone had come to inspect the place because of a reported trespasser, that would be the first place they'd look.

The rotting staircase wasn't a good choice either. I doubted it would hold my weight.

I had no choice. I edged over the counter and prepared to dive behind it the moment the door opened.

But it didn't.

I waited a full five minutes, but nothing happened. No one came in.

Was the person still out there? Were they planning on coming in? What were they waiting for?

Slowly, I eased back up to the windows, attempting to see if the person had left or not. The door, being recessed into the face of the building, and the cracks in the slats being what they were, made it hard to view from my angle. I couldn't see anyone within the door frame, but someone was there for sure. Cigarette smoke curled up from out of the recess.

Whoever it was, they were watching the wrestling club, just as I had been doing.

Realizing that whoever was standing outside had no interest in coming into the building, I relaxed some. The person remained hidden behind the door frame. Smoke continued to curl into the air.

Nearly twenty minutes passed.

Then, through the glass, I heard footsteps approaching from the westbound sidewalk.

"About time you got here," growled the waiting man outside the door, startling me. His voice was gravelly and deep, like the chugging crunch of a jackhammer.

I glimpsed the approaching man as he hopped up the steps of the front stoop to join the one who had been waiting. He appeared to be carrying something at his side, but I couldn't tell what. I also didn't catch the second man's face, but something about his form and movements looked familiar, like maybe I'd met him before.

"I've been waiting for over an hour," complained the first man with the gravelly voice.

I knew that to be an exaggeration, but I wasn't about to go out there and correct him.

"You've been standing here for an hour?" snapped the second man. His voice was softer, with a whining texture to it. "That was stupid. Someone could've seen you."

"Who cares?"

"I care! The place is crawling with cops."

"So what? Nobody knows me from Adam."

"That doesn't matter? One of them could've grown suspicious and come over to question you. Asked for ID."

"No one did. And besides, nothing is happening over there. It's a snooze-fest. No one in or out."

"Still, the least you could've done was wait for me inside."

"Whaddya mean inside? Inside where?"

"Look at the chain, you idiot. The building's unlocked."

Uh-oh.

They had noticed the opened lock. There was a good chance the two men were about to come inside.

As nimbly as possible, I leaped across the floor towards the back counter. And sure enough, the door rattled behind me. I was just diving for cover when the door screeched open and the two men bounded inside. I heard the door slam shut and the jangling of the chain that I'd unlatched earlier.

I was trapped.

———◦———

18

I HUDDLED BEHIND THE counter as still as stone, wondering if I was going to have to fight my way out of this place. I had no view of the two men, but I wasn't about to peek and expose myself. I scanned the area behind the counter, looking for a weapon, anything to use for protection if confronted. The only thing available was an empty wine bottle about five feet away. I refrained from reaching for it, however, preferring instead to remain still and quiet.

"For future reference," growled the man with the gravelly voice, "I don't like being called an idiot."

"I only meant that we need to be…aw, forget about it."

"What happened to you? You look pretty messed up."

"I'm okay. I just need to go home and change."

"You look like crap."

"I'm okay."

"What was this place, a restaurant?"

"How should I know?"

I heard footsteps wandering on the other side of the counter.

"Well, look at all the chairs and—"

"What does it matter?" snapped the second man. "At least we're off the street."

"But why would it be unlocked? The chain dangling that way?" wondered Gravelly-voice.

"Who knows? Kids. Vandals. Maybe someone forgot to lock up."

"Maybe. Just weird is all."

"When did you arrive?"

"This morning around eight."

I heard the scratch of a match against the counter, and the intake of someone lighting a cigarette. They were just on the other side of my hiding place.

"You have the ticket as I asked?" asked the softer voiced man.

"Yeah, here it is. I still don't see why you want it."

"That's my business."

"You know it's no good anymore, right?"

"Maybe not to you."

"Whatever." Footsteps moved away from the counter toward the front of the building. "It looks like we can still watch the place through the cracks in the boards." It was Gravelly-voice.

"Have you seen him come out yet?"

"As I said before, no one's gone in or come out."

"The police are probably still questioning everyone inside."

"Even if the guy had come out, what good would've it done me? I don't even know what he looks like."

"Oh right, I forgot...I've got a photograph of him somewhere."

I heard a muffled snap and the sound of someone rummaging through papers. I now realized that the object the man had been carrying must have been a briefcase.

"Here," said the second man. "It's an old promotional picture from years ago, but that's him."

"Hmm...tough guy, huh?"

"You could say that. I would be careful if I were you. He's big. And mean."

"Ooh, I'm scared." The man chuckled with his gravelly voice.

"Just don't get too close."

"Well, I have to get somewhat close, don't I? Otherwise..."

"Whatever. I'm just warning you."

"Say, while you got that thing open, why don't you give me the papers now."

"I don't have them here."

"Well, why not?"

"Because I didn't want to be walking around with them on me."

"Then why am I here?"

"You're here to help fix things. You know what you're supposed to do."

"Yeah, I know what I'm supposed to do. But I was told to bring the papers back with me too."

"Look across the street!" yelled the second man. "There is no way I'm going in there to get them right now!"

"Okay, okay...calm down. It's just that you-know-who will not be happy if I come back empty-handed."

"I'll mail the papers later after things cool down."

"He's not going to like it."

"Well, if he wants the deal to go through, it will have to do."

"They're good to go? Signed and everything?"

"Yes, they are good to go."

"She sign them too?"

"Yes, of course, but everything is post-dated, so you have to fix our problem by tomorrow or they're no good at all."

The gravelly-voiced man snorted. "Don't worry, I'll take care of everything."

"I hope so, otherwise I'm..." The second man paused as if he didn't want to finish the sentence. "Look, I've got to get going, I haven't been home yet."

"Why not?"

"I couldn't go home until you got here, now could I?" he snapped. "I had to wait it out. Don't be stupid."

A sudden hush fell over the room. Even from behind the counter, I could feel the tension between the two men intensify. One of them took in a heavy breath.

"I'll tell you what," spoke the gravelly-voiced man, but in a soft tone that somehow strengthened the menace of his words. "You don't know me very well...us being new acquaintances and all. But I don't care for being called 'stupid' by nobody—and that's the second time you've done it. You do it again, and you won't have to worry about your problem anymore. You won't have to worry about any problems at all. Are you catching my drift?"

"Y...yes. I'm sorry. I apologize. No need to get touchy. It's been a long night. I just want to go home and go to sleep."

"Then go. I got it from here. And it would be best for everyone if you could get me those papers before I leave. You catch my drift?"

"I...I don't see how I can...at least, not until tomorrow morning."

"I'm leaving around nine in the morning. Just get them to me before then and we'll be okay."

"I...I'll do my best. But I can't make any promises."

A long pause filled the room. The tension was still there. Finally, Gravelly-voice said:

"Go home. I got a picture of the dude now. I got your home phone number. I'll call you when it's done."

I heard feet shuffling toward the door. The hinges creaked. The door shut. I remained hunkered down, listening. The room had fallen quiet. My knees were hurting from kissing the tiled floor. I was about to come up from behind the counter when a voice mumbled from across the room, stopping me cold.

"Call me stupid, will ya? I'll put you in the ground, you stupid kite."

The gravelly-voiced man was still here.

Another match was struck, and immediately I smelled cigarette smoke wafting through the room. My knees were killing me and my lower legs were falling asleep. I remained still for another ten minutes.

Then I heard the man mutter to himself, "There you are! Just like your picture. Had to come out sooner or later, didn't you?"

Twenty seconds later, the hinges of the door creaked open, and the door slammed shut again. Easing my head up from behind the counter, I could see that I was now alone.

Stretching to full height, I hobbled with my prickly limbs over to the windows. Just as I peered through the slats, a figure, who I assumed was Gravelly-voice, bounded down the stoop to disappear down the sidewalk.

Across the street, I spotted a man in a blue suit maneuvering around the saw-horse barriers as if just coming through the front doors of the Knickerbocker Wrestling Federation. It seemed he had paused to light a cigarette, which now dangled from his lips. A big guy, he looked to be in his forties.

I waited twenty seconds—long enough for the man who had just left the abandoned building to be well down the block. Then, slowly, I cracked open the door. I did my best to keep the sound of the rusty hinges at a minimum, just in case Mr. Gravelly-voice was loitering about outside.

The stoop was empty, so I stepped out and peeked around the edge of the door frame. The man with the gravelly voice was fleeing after the man in the blue suit at a steady trot. He wore a gray suit and black hat and was cutting across the street to fall in behind the other man. As he reached the other sidewalk, he took a final drag on his cigarette and tossed it into the gutter.

What was his business with the man? Why was he following him?

I hadn't yet processed the conversation that I'd been privy to—the one between the two men inside the abandoned building—but it didn't take a genius to know that they knew something about the situation across the street and intended ill-will for someone associated with the building. Possibly someone connected to the wrestling club. The first man had been waiting for the man in the blue suit to come out of the building.

Was this the 'problem' that needed to be taken care of?

There was no time to think it through. I needed to act now. It was my only lead.

I eased down the steps of the stoop; I gave a cautious glance toward the front of the wrestling club. Still no cops outside. I turned and hustled after the gravelly-voiced man in the black hat. And, I suppose in a sense, the man in the blue suit too.

———◆———

19

I HAD YET TO see the face of the man wearing the gray suit and black hat, but he was about my size, just under six feet tall, about one seventy. He had a confident strut, as if tailing someone was a common occurrence for him.

The other man, the one in the blue suit, was larger—I could tell from even a block away. He was a slab of a man, with wide shoulders and a thick neck. He had to be at least six-four or five, and well over two hundred pounds. I had caught a fleeting glimpse of his profile as he'd left the wrestling club. He looked to be in his forties, and for a big guy, his movements were nimble, yet with a sense of force behind them. A wrestler. Or maybe a boxer.

I hung back, keeping at least a half a block behind Mr. Gravelly-voice. Up ahead, the man in the blue suit had turned the corner. Gone. But the man wearing the black hat remained in my sights.

Soon he, too, disappeared around the corner and I trotted to catch up.

The cross street was much busier, and with the sidewalks full of afternoon pedestrians, it was easy to blend. Mr. Gravelly-voice never looked back to check for a tail, so that made it easier still. Our little parade kept going for a couple more blocks. That's when the Slab-man at the head of the parade ducked into a Woolworth's Five and Dime Store.

Gravelly-voice hesitated, as if deliberating whether or not to go in after him.

I slowed my pace. Watching.

After half a minute, Gravelly-voice also entered Woolworth's.

Now it was my turn to pause on the sidewalk. Should I follow in after them? I had no idea who these two characters were, what they were up to, or if they were connected to Manny Greenstreet and his murder. I could be batting at windmills.

Frustrated, I shrugged, thinking that, as far as leads go, this was the best I had.

I came through the doors of Woolworth's to find a lunch counter running along the left-hand wall and a handful of red-vinyl booths on the right. At the counter, several customers sat atop swiveling stools with stainless steel pedestals. Gravelly-voice was one of them—I recognized his black hat and gray suit. He sat about four stools down, hunched, with his elbows on the counter. A waitress had just placed a cup and saucer in front of him and was pouring him coffee from a carafe.

He slanted a look my way as I hesitated at the entryway. Our eye-lines clashed for a split second. There was no sense of recognition in the glare, but I thought I caught a hint of suspicion.

He had an angular, unshaven jaw, a scowling mouth, and dark eyes that squinted with malice.

To my left, I spotted an empty stool where the counter elbowed around to meet the wall, so I sat down, trying to look relaxed. Fortunately, the seat was well-positioned to take in the rest of the room.

The vinyl-covered booths on the right were all empty except for two; an older couple sat in one at the far end, and halfway down a woman with dark hair sat alone in the other.

The slab-man in the blue suit was nowhere to be found.

The lunch area was glassed off from the rest of Woolworth's, with a door at the far end of the lunchroom leading into the store. Had Slab-man gone into the store?

Through the glass, I could see a herd of shoppers and a handful of clerks attending to customers, but I saw no sign of him. So where had he gone? And why was Gravelly-voice still here? Did he lose track of the man?

Or had he spotted me tailing him and decided to check me out instead?

A waitress was suddenly in front of me with an order pad and pencil. She wore a clean uniform under a crisp white apron and had a mirthful smile between cherry cheeks.

"What can I get you, sir?"

I ordered a chocolate soda. She wrote it down and turned away.

In my peripheral vision, I sensed Gravelly-voice watching me. I made it a point not to look directly at him. I was suddenly feeling paranoid about being on his radar.

I felt flummoxed. None of this made sense. Gravelly-voice had stopped following Slab-man for some reason. Why? Had he lost him? Or had the other man given us both the slip?

Then a new thought occurred to me. Maybe Gravelly-voice had been following someone else all along. Had another person come out of the wrestling club I hadn't noticed? But even if that was the case, the man in the blue suit had somehow vanished. But to where?

And then...

I saw him...or at least, I thought I did.

At the end of the lunch counter, down near the door leading into the store, were two phone booths side-by-side. The doors to both booths were closed, but through the smoky glass of one of them, I could see the form of a man talking on the telephone. Was it Slab-man? Possibly. There was only one way to find out: sit and wait for him to come out.

My soda came. The thought occurred to me that if Slab-man were to come out of the booth and leave the lunchroom, we all might make a hasty exit to take up our parade again. I pulled some change out of my pocket and found a dime for the drink. Feeling generous, I placed another dime on the counter as a tip for the cherry-cheeked waitress—a 100% tip. Not bad.

Nonchalantly, I kept my eye on the telephone booth but avoided looking Gravelly-voice's way. I couldn't tell if he was watching me or not. It worried me some that he might be studying my face. If we started up our little parade again, Gravelly-voice might be more aware of being tailed this time.

The man possessed a threatening aura. I could feel it from across the lunch counter, like bottled rage. It made me nervous. Even during the conversation that I'd overhead in the abandoned building, and without seeing him, I'd sensed how dangerous the man could be—the other man in the conversation had known it too. I sensed it even more from ten feet away.

I was taking my first sip of the soda when the doors to the phone booth swiveled open and the man inside stepped out.

20

IT WAS SLAB-MAN OKAY—SAME build, same blue suit.

Gravelly-voice took notice of the clatter that the phone booth door had made and slid a glance that way, keeping track of his prey in a low key manner.

The man stepping from the booth had black wavy hair that was slicked back on his head with pomade; a few strands fell across his forehead. A heavy, Neanderthal brow shadowed dark eyes, and his nose looked to have been busted a time or two. For being a large and intimidating man, he looked somewhat beaten down, as if he'd had a bad day and it wasn't getting any better.

Recalling tidbits of Gus's story from last night and this morning—as well as my conversation with Nick at the gym—it came to me that Slab-man might be Manny Greenstreet's partner, Mickey Jacobs. The description fit.

The man stepped over and paused next to one of the red-vinyl booths—the one with the woman sitting by herself. She must have known him, for she smiled up at him—albeit woefully—and reached up to take his hand. He attempted to smile, but it became more of a grimace than a smile. He took a seat across from her and she continued to stroke his hand in a consoling manner.

I could only see the back of his slick head now, but I had a good view of the woman. She was a pretty brunette with thick wavy hair tossed off to the side, like Greta Garbo. Her lips were full and gleaming with red lipstick. Her eyes were ultramarine blue and soulful, sympathetic. But one of her eyes looked off. The eye socket appeared to be darker than the other, as if she were sporting a black eye and had slathered on make-up to cover it up. Dressed in a powder-blue smock with a silver necklace, she had a suitable set of shoulders, as well as a suitable set of breasts—both emphasized by a straight-backed posture.

Staring at her, and the way she was built, and considering the possible black-eye, I had to wonder if this could be the female wrestler that Gus had told me about—the one who dressed up as a nurse. If that was the case, I had to admit, even I would pay to watch her wrestle another woman.

The two of them talked in low tones, but I was too far away to hear anything of their discussion. I couldn't say the same for Mr. Gravely-voice. He was closer, but remained unaffected as he huddled over his coffee cup. He looked neither at them nor at me.

The couple then opened the menus that had been laying on the table and a waitress bounced over to the booth to take their order. I could tell that they were making choices that went beyond mere coffee. It appeared our little parade was pausing for lunch. Having only eaten a bag of peanuts all day, I figured that if they were going to eat, I might as well, too. I summoned the cherry-cheeked waitress, who was working the counter, and ordered a chicken salad sandwich.

Gravelly-voice appeared content with his coffee. He continued his sullen vigil.

I sipped at my soda and watched the room, wondering where this was going to take me, and if it was going to help keep Gus out of jail.

I had a few minutes to kill as we waited for our meals to arrive, so I decided to place a call to Nick Terrano. It had been a couple of hours since I'd left the gym and he had promised to make some calls around town, asking about this Mickey Jacobs character. Maybe he'd have some news for me.

I left my stool at the counter, and headed for the phone booths at the other end, bisecting a path between both players in our little melodrama,

Slab-man in the booth on the right and Gravelly-voice at the lunch-counter on the left. I avoided eye contact with both parties.

Entering one of the phone booths, I slipped a nickel into the slot and got an operator on the line. I gave her Nick's number.

"I'm glad you called Buck," said Nick when he came on the line. "I've found out some interesting things about Manny Greenstreet and his partnership with Mickey Jacobs. It seems the two of them were on the outs with each other. Greenstreet apparently, wanted to expand their little wrestling empire into other cities. He even went out to Chicago a couple of weeks ago to explore franchise opportunities and to begin talks with some people out there about opening up offices and arranging for shows in the mid-west."

"That's probably what he was doing when he came across Gus in Minneapolis," I said.

"Could be. But I found out one interesting bit of information."

"What's that?"

"Something of a turf-war got started. And Greenstreet and Jacobs were at odds about it."

"What do you mean, turf-war?"

"There's another wrestling outfit in town. It's twice as big as the Knickerbocker Club and also their chief competition."

"Which outfit is that?"

"The Greater Manhattan Wrestling Federation. From what I've been told, they're large enough to have franchises in other cities."

"Like Chicago?"

"Exactly. And the word on the street is that they wanted to buy out the Knickerbocker Club here in New York and had made an offer to both partners."

"So what were Greenstreet and Jacobs at odds about?"

"Manny Greenstreet wanted to hold on to their ownership stake and grow their operation. Mickey Jacobs wanted to cash out. From what I heard, he was already in talks with the other outfit about buying the Knickerbocker Club lock, stock, and barrel—including all of their wrestlers."

Which meant Gus too, I thought, unless I could still get his contract back—and if I could keep him out of prison, otherwise the contract was moot.

"Who runs that other club?" I asked.

"Fella by the name of Big Bob Barton."

"Never heard of him."

"He's a former wrestler himself. Used to wrestle under the name of Boulder Bart. The guy weighs over three hundred pounds. Mean SOB. One of my guys told me he once killed a guy in the ring by sitting on his face and smothering him to death."

"Let me guess, they charged him with first-degree man-squatter."

"Huh?"

I waited for Nick to catch up to the joke, but then remembered that Nick is nearly humorless.

"Nah, they didn't charge Barton with anything. Just like boxers, those guys sign waivers, and all that crap. Everyone looked at it as an accidental death. Besides, from what my sources say, there was little to no chance of charges being brought on account of Barton being connected."

"Connected? As in the mob?"

"Yeah, the Jewish mob, Meyer Lansky's group."

I cringed at the mention of the infamous Jewish mobster. Lansky was known for eliminating people who got in his way. It was common knowledge that a few years ago, back in '31, Lansky and his friends, Bugsy Siegel and Lucky Luciano, had two of the most powerful Italian Mafia bosses in the country gunned down—Joe Masseria and Salvatore Maranzano—just a couple of guys who got in their way. Talk about a turf-war.

"You think Lansky is involved with Barton's wrestling club?"

"As I understand it, The Greater Manhattan Wrestling Federation has the backing of the Jewish mob. Whether Lansky himself is personally involved, I couldn't tell you."

If those guys were involved in the wrestling game, who knows to what extent they'd go to protect their interests.

"You think Greenstreet could've been a hit?" I asked.

"I wouldn't want to guess," said Nick, as if afraid to even speculate. "All I know is that Big Bob Barton and the Greater Manhattan club wanted to buy the Knickerbocker club, and Greenstreet didn't want to sell."

"And Mickey Jacobs did."

"Bingo."

I thought about that for a moment. Had Greenstreet angered the mob with his reticence? Could his murder have been a mob hit? People like Lansky certainly didn't like people standing in their way. However, it didn't quite make sense.

I pictured in my mind the scene inside Greenstreet's office last night, his bashed-in head, the blood spatter, and his broken glasses off to the side. Was that the work of the mob? They were violent for sure, but mob hits tend to go down with bullets, not with desk legs. Two taps in the back of the head was more the style of the Jewish mob, or just a disappearance altogether. Yet Greenstreet had been taken out by blunt force trauma.

Another image flashed through my brain. The image of Gus putting Murphy down on the canvas with one punch. Blunt force! A guy Gus's size could do a lot of damage with a desk leg. Especially if he was angry. I shook away the image. It couldn't have been Gus...right?

I glanced through the glass of the phone booth to where Mickey Jacobs was sitting with the brunette. He was about Gus's size too, maybe bigger. No doubt he could do damage wielding a desk leg.

"Is Mickey Jacobs made?" I asked.

"How would I know?" snorted Nick in a somewhat offended tone. "Even if I was connected—which I'm not—it wouldn't be with the Jews. I'm Italian." He hesitated. "Are you thinking that maybe Jacobs killed Manny?"

"Possibly. If the two were at odds and there was money to be made, he had the most to gain."

"If Mickey's behind this, I doubt he was anywhere near Greenstreet's office. He'd have an alibi in the bag."

Nick was probably right about that. But that didn't completely absolve him. He could have paid to have it done. And if he truly was in bed with the likes of Lansky, Siegel, and Luciano, then any number of goons would be at his disposal to take out his partner—yes, even by blunt force trauma.

Nick said, "I also want to remind you of what I said earlier about Jacobs. He can be dangerous. He has a temper like gasoline."

"That's a character flaw that benefits us," I said. "It adds to his motive."

"Even so, it would be healthy for you to stay away from him."

"That's a little hard to do at the moment," I replied.

"What do you mean?"

"I'm looking right at him."

"What? Where are you?" he cried. He sounded panicked.

"I'm at Woolworth's by Union Square eating lunch, and Jacobs is sitting in a booth twenty feet away."

"Dammit, Buck, if Jacobs was willing to take out his partner, he's not even going to blink over killing you."

I was watching Jacobs with his woman friend. I now had a view of his face. At the moment, he didn't look dangerous at all. Yes, he was a large man, with a brooding face, square jaw, and a crooked nose, but he also looked grim and troubled, as if his life had just gone off the rails. Was it from losing his partner, or was something else bothering him?

"Mickey Jacobs doesn't even know I exist," I answered into the receiver.

"Stay clear!" he ordered.

To change the topic, I asked Nick about Gus.

"He's doing fine. I found a set of sweats in a locker and he's been working out—letting off steam. The guy has moves. I might put him in the ring later to do some sparring."

"With Murphy?"

Nick grunted. "Naw, Murph left early today. He was pretty upset—and humiliated. I don't think he's too eager to climb into the ring with the Swede anytime soon."

"Well, thanks Nick for the information," I said. "I'll give you another call later when—"

I stopped in mid-sentence. A giant man had just lumbered through the front doors of Woolworth's, causing an eerie tingle to flit up my spine. He sported a three hundred dollar suit and gold flashed from his fingers and wrists. Arrogance radiated from him like heat. A huge man, his bulk filled the doorway.

If any man on earth could wear the nickname *Boulder* effectively...this was the guy.

21

NICK'S VOICE CAME THROUGH the receiver. "You still there, Buck?"

"Yeah, I'm still here."

I was taking in the man at the other end of the lunchroom. He was mountain-like. He stood at least six-six, with a Buddha belly that bulged through the opening of his tailored suit coat. His head was shaved bald and came to a dull point at the crown, giving the impression of a mammoth bullet emerging from his shoulders. Hostility racked his face; he had mean eyes and a scowl for a mouth. Two men came in behind him, shifty-looking characters dressed in dark suits. They hovered behind him, scanning the Woolworth lunch crowd with scrutiny.

The big man went straight to the booth where Mickey Jacobs sat. The other two men took seats across the way at the counter, just down from where Gravelly-voice sat.

I still held the telephone earpiece in my hand.

"Say, Nick, what does this Big Bob Barton look like?"

Nick described him.

"I'm looking at him," I said.

"He's there? At Woolworth's?"

"In the flesh—and I'm talking a lot of flesh. He's sitting down with Mickey Jacobs as we speak."

"What are you going to do?"

"I haven't decided yet."

"Buck!" Nick yelled. "If Jacobs is gasoline, that guy is nitroglycerin. Remember what I said about him being connected to Lansky. You need to get out of there before—"

I hung up before he could finish.

I walked back to my seat with my head down, avoiding eye contact with those sitting in the booth as I passed.

My food was waiting for me. I unfolded a napkin and placed it over my lap. After taking a sip from my chocolate soda, I grabbed one half of my chicken salad sandwich. I was just about to bite into it when I sensed movement along the lunch counter. Taking a casual glance that way, I saw Mr. Gravelly-voice climbing down from his stool as he tossed change on the counter-top. Lunchtime was over for him. He turned and headed for the exit behind me. It seems the presence of Big Bob and his henchmen disturbed him for some reason. However, he didn't rush out; he sauntered with confidence.

I kept him in my peripheral view.

I could've been wrong, but as he passed by, I thought I caught him sneaking a look at me. An unhappy, suspicious look that made me squirm.

For a moment, I felt conflicted. Gravelly-voice had left. Why? Had he seen enough? Or had Big Bob Barton and his crew scared him off?

But the bigger question was, should I follow him? Or should I stick with this new cast of characters?

Barton had squeezed into the booth next to the brunette so that he was facing Jacobs. I had a good view of him. Eye candy, he was not. He made for a threatening presence. Hulking, obese, and ugly enough to make my skin crawl.

I decided to stay and finish my lunch and watch the meeting unfolding before my eyes. The heck with Gravelly-voice. He was on his own now. I figured the people in the booth were closer to the situation and my best bet at figuring out who killed Manny Greenstreet.

They talked in hushed tones. From where I sat, I couldn't hear their conversation, but the optics were such that it did not seem like a cordial discussion. Barton said little; his eyes said it all. His glare was scorching. With Mickey Jacob's back to me, I couldn't see his demeanor, but his arms gestured as if offering an explanation or possibly defending himself against an accusation. Either way, the scowl on Big Bob's face told me he wasn't happy with the turn of the conversation.

I was so intent on trying to listen in that I found myself leaning across the countertop, sandwich in hand, while cocking my head in an attempt to overhear the conversation.

Big mistake.

Being focused on Jacobs and Barton, I had failed to notice that the pretty brunette sitting with them was shooting me a curious squint. When I suddenly realized it, our eyes locked. It was too late. She had caught me trying to eavesdrop.

We stared at each other for a few seconds. Her eyebrows arched, her eyes questioning. Then, strangely, a smile curled up into her face, a tiny dimple forming in her cheek. Her chin arched with something of a knowing look gracing her face.

That's when I realized something. This was the same woman who had come out of the wrestling building earlier. The one with the confident smile that I had appreciated.

And now she directed that confident smile my way.

Was she flirting with me?

She gave a cock of her head toward Jacobs, her knowing smile in place, but her eyes trained on me. It almost felt like a signal. As if she were saying, 'too bad, but I'm with him.'

That was her mistake.

Jacobs must have caught the slight motion, or her wandering attention, for I heard him growl and the conversation at the table abruptly ended. She snapped her focus away from me and back to him, blinking as he mumbled something to her.

Her red lips moved in a low whisper.

Mickey Jacob's head twisted a look over his shoulder at me. I nearly choked on my sandwich. His glare had wrath attached.

Big Bob Barton's eyes sliced my way, too.

I didn't enjoy being the center of attention.

I attempted a quick bit of acting, pretending to glance around, taking in the other patrons of the restaurant, and smiling at the waitress. But it didn't fly. The three of them put their heads together for a quick huddle. As they all backed out of the huddle, Big Bob gave a tick of his head—didn't say a word, just ticked—and suddenly the two goons who had come in with him had slipped away from their stools at the counter and were now standing behind me.

"Let's go," one of them snorted.

It happened quickly, so quickly that I hadn't time to swallow my mouthful of chicken salad. In an instant, I went from a passive observer to being hip deep with the Jewish mob.

"Go where?" I asked, my cheek bulging with food.

"Big Bob wants to talk to you."

"I don't know anyone by that name."

"Just get up."

"No thanks. If you don't mind, I need to finish lunch so I can get back to the office."

"Get up," he repeated. It wasn't a request.

———————— ❧ ————————

22

THE OTHER FELLOW GRABBED my jacket at the back of my neck and lifted me from my stool. My shirt and tie constricted my throat, and I coughed up the food in my mouth. Hard to look cool when that happens. They dragged me down the length of the counter as the other patrons swiveled to watch in astonishment. The cherry-cheeked waitress behind the counter blinked with open-mouthed puzzlement.

"Nothing to see here," grunted one of the goons. And everyone quickly turned back to their meals.

Once we reached the booth, the one guy continued to hold me by the neck, as the other patted me down for weapons. He found the pliers I'd bought earlier and tossed them on the table. Big Bob cocked his head with curiosity at the sight.

"Those aren't loaded," I said.

No one laughed.

The guy frisking me found my wallet in my jacket pocket, took it out, and handed it to Big Bob. Then they shoved me into the booth, squeezing me in next to Mickey Jacobs. I could smell his aftershave.

One brave customer sitting at the counter had grown curious, or Good Samaritan-like, and had turned around again as if to intercede. One goon quickly addressed him:

"You got a problem, pal?" He growled, puffing his chest in front of the customer.

The man opened his mouth to speak, thought better of it, and went back to nibbling on his BLT. The goons returned to their stools next to him.

The diner became deathly quiet.

"Say, what's this about?" I asked, all shocked and indignant. "I just came in for a chicken salad sandwich and—"

"Shut-up," said Big Bob Barton in a soft, hoarse whisper, his lips barely rippling. He was busy looking through my wallet, not finding much. I keep nothing in it to identify myself. And I only carry small amounts of cash, but he didn't seem interested in the money.

Up close, he was frightening to look at. Tiny cruel eyes, half-lidded, set wide in his bullet-shaped head, his jaw flexed over a jowly neck. His movements were minimal, controlled, but I could feel malice radiating from his skin.

"This the guy?" he asked with a glance at Jacobs.

Mickey Jacobs was leering at me.

"Could be. I saw him hanging outside the building across the street earlier today. When I came out, he must have followed me here."

I gulped, wondering what he meant by that. But then I realized. He was mistaking me for Gravelly-voice, who had made no effort to be discrete. I also realized how, from a distance, that mistake could easily be made. I was about the same size as Gravelly-voice, and—although I hadn't thought of it before now—the two of us were dressed alike. Gray suit, black fedora.

"What's your game, fella?" asked Barton. "Why are you following Mickey here?"

He continued sifting through my wallet.

"Hey, I wasn't following anyone," I pleaded. "I just came in to eat lunch. And like I told your friends, I need to get back to the office. It's that time of year...you know how it is, Consolidated is merging with Amalgamated."

He pierced me with a glare that told me to shut my mouth.

"How convenient...no ID," he mumbled. "Not much of anything in his wallet."

But then Barton paused with a probing squint. His fat fingers reached into the flaps of the wallet and pulled out a piece of paper he'd found. And my heart nearly stopped.

It was the home address for Mickey Jacobs that Nick Terrano had written down for me.

Barton read off the address.

"Hey, that's my place," yelped Jacobs.

Barton's eyes hardened on me. "Don't know him, huh?"

I remained quiet.

"Did Chicago send you?" he asked.

"What?" I managed to say.

"Chicago!" he repeated. "You from Chi-town?"

"Why would he be from Chicago?" interjected the woman? "What do they have to do with anything?"

"Shut-up," said Barton without looking at her.

The woman was studying me, I could tell. Her ultramarine eyes had an inquisitive but guarded aspect. Now that I was closer, I could tell that she had indeed tried to cover a black-eye with make-up.

"Answer my question!" barked Barton. "Are you from Chicago?"

"I'm from New York. I've never stepped foot outside the five boroughs."

"You a wop? You don't look Italian." He peered over at Jacobs. "He look like a wop to you?"

"No," replied Jacobs, summing me up. "He looks like a mick to me."

"A mick?" sneered Barton. "A lot of micks are cops. You a cop?"

I felt insulted by that remark—much more so than being called a wop—but I kept it to myself.

"No," I said.

"So why are you following Mickey here?" He gave a tick of the head toward Jacobs.

I glanced over at him. "I don't know this man. And I certainly haven't been following him."

"Then why is his address in your wallet?"

I had no explanation for that other than the truth, and I wasn't ready to spill that just yet, so I didn't answer. I thought about running. My eyes drifted over to the two guys sitting on stools across the way. They were watching me. I would never make it to the door.

"Don't look at them," snorted Barton. "Look at me. And don't even think about turning rabbit. My guys will break you in two."

I remained silent.

"I'm going to ask you again. Did Chicago send you?"

"I have no idea what you are talking about, sir." I thought it might help my position to talk like Gus. And for a brief second, it did. Barton blinked with confusion, as if he wasn't used to being addressed respectfully.

"Look, if you're here to stop the deal. It's too late. It's going through anyway. I know Bomberg talked to the wops in Chicago, but our deal here is solid."

I shifted in my seat, wondering who Bomberg could be.

"Bomberg knows the score," continued Barton. "He was there during the talks. We had a deal. But if he's planning a double-cross because he wants to throw in with the Italians, he's gonna be sorry. Our guys in New York don't take to being double-crossed too good."

Our guys in New York.

I didn't like the sound of that.

I recalled my conversation with Nick and how Barton was connected to Lansky. The morbid thought leaked into my cranium that there was a possibility that I might get disappeared, mob-style. True, there were no broken desk legs available, but I could envision Big Bob easily ripping up one of those chrome lunch stools and using it as a weapon.

It made me wonder where *he* had been last night when Greenstreet got whacked.

"So I'm going to ask you again, Mr. No ID. Who are you? And who sent you?"

"No one sent me. I'm just a guy who came in for a sandwich."

He leaned in closer, his face contorted, teeth flashing. "You think I'm afraid of the likes of you? You scrawny little runt." He jammed a finger into my chest. "You don't even carry a rod—just pliers. What the hell do you think you were going to do with a pair of pliers?"

"I had a loose screw that needed fixing."

"Funny guy." He simmered for a moment, watching me as he ground his teeth. "Someone sent you. It had to be Chicago. Maybe to get Mickey here to turn, maybe to keep an eye on Greenstreet."

"Green Street? I don't know how to get to Green Street from here. But if you could draw a map, I—"

The slap came out of nowhere. Didn't even see it coming. For a big man, Barton was lightning-quick. Brutal. It thundered and echoed off the diner walls. My head almost tumbled from my shoulder.

"Shut-up," Barton mumbled, almost too soft to hear. Or maybe it was my ears ringing. "Don't act dumb with me."

We stared at each other for a year or two. I could feel the blood rushing to my cheek. I'd be wearing his fingerprints for a while. Across the table, the pretty brunette blinked with shock, maybe fear. The atmosphere in the diner entered an ice age. They had all heard the slap, too. No one moved.

"Don't act like you don't know who Greenstreet is. If Chicago sent you to babysit him, you're too late. He's a non-factor now."

"What do you mean, a non-factor?" I mumbled. My jaw still throbbing.

Barton leaned in closer. "A. Non. Fact. Tor."

"Look," I said. "I'm just a guy taking a lunch break. I don't know you and I don't know anyone named Bomberg."

"Then why are you always where I'm at?" asked Mickey Jacobs, sitting next to me.

"Coincidence," I offered, but I didn't look his way. Big Bob had my full attention.

Barton hunched his shoulders over the table, his immensity casting a shadow over the dishes. "I don't believe in coincidences."

I stayed quiet, watching for his slapping hand.

"A guy comes in, no ID, tailing my friend, has his home address in his wallet. That's no coincidence. It makes me think he's got his nose up in my business."

"I don't even know what your business is," I replied with as much humility as I could muster.

"Why don't I believe you?"

"I don't know. I'm told I have a very trusting face."

This time, I did see it coming. I threw my hands up in surrender. The slap hesitated in mid-air.

"Trusting face," he snarled. His hand eased back down to the table, and for a second, I was relieved. But he then let loose a thin whistle, and the two goons were suddenly standing at the booth. Like junkyard dogs being summoned.

"I'm getting sick of this guy." He wadded up the paper with Jacob's address on it, folded my wallet, and jammed it into my jacket pocket. The pliers he handed to one of the goons.

"I keep asking questions and getting the same answer. Take this mick somewhere and make adjustments to his trusting face. Use the pliers."

The brunette gasped.

"But sir, I like my face the way it is," I offered.

However, the 'sir' thing just wasn't working. Big Bob's lips curled back in a sneer. His half-lidded eyes went dead and pitiless. I guess only kids from the mid-west can pull off the 'yes sir/no sir' thing.

The goons lifted me from my seat. I felt something hard poke my ribs. I looked down and found a gun there. I couldn't tell if it was a .38 or a .45. Either way, it was wrinkling my jacket.

"Let's go outside," said the goon with the gun. An ugly smile curled up into his face. I could tell he was the type to enjoy working a guy over with pliers.

They twisted me around, shoving me toward the exit.

That's when the street doors burst open and...

...my newest best friend in the world came striding into Woolworth's.

———◆———

23

"Freeze, Bucky!" yelled Detective Wilbur Crenshaw from Woolworth's doorway.

I did.

The goons, however, didn't.

Yes, they hesitated, but only for a split second. Then, smelling cop-stink like bloodhounds, the gun in my side vanished, and both men melted back onto their stools at the counter. Actions that nearly made me giddy.

"You and I need to talk," spit Crenshaw. He came at me full trot, his dopey face red with rage.

From the booth to my left, I heard Jacobs mumbling under his breath, "That's the cop that grilled us this morning."

"Shut-up," Big Bob snarled, and the booth went quiet.

Crenshaw squared himself in front of me, his eyes glued to my face. It left me chagrined and relieved at once. Little did he know he'd become my—savior. I could've kissed him.

"Wilbur, you don't know how happy I am to see y—"

"Shut-up," he barked.

"But I just wanted to tell you about—"

"Out!" he yelled. "Now!"

The lunch crowd stared.

Grabbing my lapel, Crenshaw jerked a thumb toward the exit. "Now!"

Being yanked toward the door, I glanced back at the thugs behind me. I shrugged to imply that the plier-torture would have to be postponed.

Big Bob Barton's glare was lethal enough to kill most of the kittens in a five-block radius.

The moment we hit the sidewalk, Crenshaw jerked me around to throw me up against Woolworth's front window, my face pressed up against the glass.

"Smile for your friends," Crenshaw muttered in my ear, hostility laced with glee.

"I have no friends in there," I said through mashed lips.

"Really? They're all watching like they care."

He was half right. Indeed, every face inside looked our way. Most with a total lack of care. Big Bob glowered. His two goons at the counter smirked. But the cherry-cheeked waitress appeared disappointed, like I'd let her down by making enemies during lunch.

Handcuffs came out and Crenshaw clamped my hands behind my back.

"Is this really necessary?" I asked, the cuffs biting into my wrists.

"This is how I handle thieves and liars."

"And I thought we were friends, Wilbur."

"Friends? Ha! You think you're something, don't you!" he hissed.

"Of course I'm something, I ain't nothing."

He yanked me around, roughly, as if doing it for show. He glanced past me toward the lunch counter crowd.

"You're keeping pretty dangerous company these days, Bucky."

"Those guys in there? We belong to the same knitting circle. We were gonna make you a scarf, but now I don't know."

"Why is it you seem to be hip deep in my investigation?"

"What investigation?"

He grit his teeth. "You lied to me this morning."

"Never."

"You kept back information about your sleepover friend."

"Who, Gus?"

"Yeah, your wrestling pal from Michigan."

"Minnesota."

"Whatever."

"And he's a boxer, not a wrestler."

"Not according to witnesses at the Knickerbocker Wrestling Federation."

"Who?"

"Don't play dumb with me, Bucky! You opened their safe last night."

"I did not."

"And you didn't tell me everything about your friend's involvement with them."

"It's not my fault you didn't ask the right questions."

Passersby paused, watching the drama. Nothing attracts a crowd like a handcuffed man. Taking note, Crenshaw grabbed me by the coat sleeve to maneuver me over to his unmarked squad car parked on the street. He opened the door and manhandled me into the back. Climbing into the front and slamming the door, he swung around to face me.

"Where's the hayseed?" he growled.

"Hayseed? That's a bit disrespectful."

His teeth flashed. "I'm in no mood for games, Bucky. I want to know where that Swedish knucklehead is and why you didn't tell me the truth about him this morning."

"I told you the truth. I said he was from Minnesota, that he was a boxer. I mentioned our evening..."

"You left out the part about the wrestling outfit."

"He wasn't wearing a wrestling outfit that I could see...maybe under his—"

"Not that kind of outfit!" He let out a snarl of exasperation. "You know damn well what I'm talking about. His association with The Knickerbocker Wrestling Federation."

"Hmm, that's the second time you've mentioned them, but I don't recall you asking about them this morning."

"I mentioned Union Square."

"Ah, that's right. You accused me of cracking a safe. I thought you were talking about a store safe, like S. Klein's. That's a store just around the corner. You didn't say a word about wrestling."

He waggled a finger at me. "You also left out the part about your friend being down here in Union Square last night."

"Was he? He didn't say so. It must have slipped his mind."

"Yeah, right. I'm sure you knew nothing about it."

I shrugged. "I suppose he could've been down here, but if you're accusing him of cracking a safe, I don't think he knows how to do that."

"Maybe not, but he knows how to beat on people, doesn't he?"

"Well, he's a boxer, so yeah."

"Where is he?"

"How should I know?"

"The last time I saw him, he was eating breakfast with you."

"We went our separate ways after that. He didn't tell me his plans. He might be halfway to St. Cloud by now."

Crenshaw turned around and started the car. "Well, let's go to your place. And if I find him there, I'm bringing you both downtown."

"For what?"

"You'll find out when I get you there."

The car lurched forward.

"How did you find me?" I asked from the back seat. It was my first ride in a cruiser; it smelled better than most taxis.

Crenshaw simmered in silence, hunched over the steering wheel as he wove through traffic. He didn't use the lights and siren, which left me disappointed. It didn't feel like an official cop car ride.

"C'mon Wilbur," I said. "It was quite a coincidence you showing up when you did. How did you know I was at Woolworth's having lunch?"

"I didn't," he muttered. "I put a tail on another guy that I had just got done questioning over at the wrestling gym. Little did I know he would lead me to you, and that the two of you would be having lunch together."

"I was eating alone, you can ask the waitress there."

"That may be so, but you ended up creating quite a scene."

"You're the one who made a scene. It was quite embarrassing."

"Oh?" His eye caught mine in the rearview mirror. "You don't call getting slapped around by Big Bob Barton making a scene?"

"You saw that?" I was stunned.

"I wish! My guy saw it from outside. He got to a phone booth and gave me an update. Being around the corner at the crime scene, I hurried over. I was curious about the mysterious idiot getting slapped around by Big Bob Barton. And surprise, surprise, it's the same idiot I'd questioned earlier this morning."

"So the fat guy's name is Big Bob, huh? That sounds about right."

"As if you didn't know. We've had our eyes on Barton for some time. He's connected to the Jewish mob, you know." He glared at me in the mirror. "That makes you connected to them too."

"I don't think so. He only slapped me for slurping my chocolate soda too loudly."

"You're lucky he didn't plug ya. He's known for that kind of stuff."

"I was glad you showed up when you did, Wilbur. His goons were about to do some damage."

"Yeah? See its statements like that, Bucky, that fills my brain box with all kinds of questions. Like, why would Big Bob care enough about a petty thief like you to even want to give you a beat down? And why would you and a guy that I just got done questioning be having lunch together? It seems implausible. I question two unrelated suspects—three, if you throw the Swede into the mix—and then I find out that all three of you know each other. And all of you are tied to Big Bob Barton and the Jewish mob."

"I'd never laid eyes on this Big Bob Barton character until half an hour ago."

"That's not how I figure it."

"No? What's your magnificent brain box telling you, Wilbur?"

"That one of those clowns you were having lunch with hired you to break into a safe last night and they weren't happy with the results. So Big Bob slaps you around to teach you a lesson."

"You're way off base."

"I don't believe in coincidences, Bucky. Everywhere I look, I see Buck Flynn eating with suspects—all of whom I can tie to an open safe."

"I wasn't eating lunch with those people. And I swear, Wilbur, I did not crack a safe last night."

"Yeah, like I can rely on the word of a known thief—especially after you lied to me this morning about Gustave Nordstrom."

"I didn't lie about—"

"Save it, Bucky!"

He studied me in the mirror. A tight smile formed on his gnome face.

"Let's ask the Swede about it when we see him, Bucky."

Wilbur jammed the cruiser into a parking spot in front of my building, got out, and swung open the back door.

After yanking me out, he said: "Turn around. If you promise to play nice, I'll take the bracelets off."

"I don't know why you put them on in the first place. I wouldn't have run, you know that, and you have nothing on me that warranted being cuffed."

"I wanted the thugs in Woolworth's to see how I treat their partner in crime."

"I am not their p—"

"Save it." He shoved me toward the front door of my building.

It felt good to have the cuffs off. If he hadn't done it, I would've taken them off myself. Pops taught me how to do it when I was six.

———◦———

24

COMING INTO THE BUILDING, we heard the elevator creaking upward. Someone was using it. Crenshaw was about to push the button to retrieve it once it deposited its passenger, but hesitated as he squinted up at its slow-motion movement. Glancing at the stairs, he gave a burdensome slump of his shoulders and waved for me to start climbing.

We plodded up the four stories. With every step, I felt his anger simmering. He mumbled things like, 'You've got some nerve jerking me around, boy' and 'I've always played fair with you and this is how I'm treated' and 'Lie to me, will you? I'll have your ass in jail'. By the time we got to my apartment, his lungs were gasping, but more from the climb than from being steamed. The climb even took some of the steam out of him. I remained silent the entire way.

The second I unlocked the door, he swept past me as if to catch Gus red-handed. But there was no Gus, of course. He did a quick and fruitless tour of my apartment. Passing by my wall of lock and key art, he scanned the display with his face twisted in disgust.

Finding no Gus regenerated his steam, which inevitably blew my way.

Planting himself in front of me, he yelped, "What did you do with him?"

"Am I my brother's keeper?"

"Where is he, Bucky?"

"I told you, we parted ways after breakfast. He's probably on a bus as we speak."

"Without his suitcase?"

"What?"

Crenshaw pointed to the cardboard suitcase leaning against the far side of my sofa.

"Oh," I croaked.

I'd forgotten all about it. So much for my cover story.

"He must have left it behind."

"Yeah, right...what kind of fool do you take me for?"

I could've answered that, but I didn't.

"You've got him stashed somewhere. Tell me where?"

I gave a wave toward the window. "I suppose he's still be here in the city someplace. Go look for him."

He growled and stomped over to grab the suitcase. He threw it up on the kitchen table, his fingers going for the clasps. I quickly stepped over and placed a hand on the suitcase lid, stopping him.

"I don't think so, Wilbur," I warned. "Not without a warrant."

Anger flashed. "Whaddaya mean warrant? You let me in here of your own volition. The law gives me the right to search."

"My own volition? You ordered me here, Wilbur. Besides, that suitcase isn't my property. I can't give you permission to open something that's not mine."

He straightened up, scowling. I could almost see the Fourth Amendment howling with laughter through his brain box.

"Without a warrant for that particular suitcase, I'm going to have to ask you to let it be. Fruit of the forbidden tree and all that."

He hitched up his trousers and tapped the brim of his fedora up on his forehead. The steam was back full throttle. "You're messing with my investigation, Bucky!" he yelled, shaking a finger my way. "And I don't like it."

"Your investigation into grand larceny? You seem pretty hot and bothered by an opened safe."

"There's more to it than that. Much more!"

"There has to be. You're so...irritated." I moved over to my icebox and opened it up. "Would you like something to drink, Wilbur?"

"No, I don't want anything to drink!" he yelled.

"That's good. Gus cleaned me out last night. The only thing I have is beer...and you are on duty, so..."

He stepped over and slammed the icebox door shut so hard it rattled the apartment. He shook his head. "I shoulda known. An empty safe. Blood on the hayseed's jacket. The two of you together all night. You were in on it together."

"In on what together? I came across a poor sap who had been mugged. I helped him out. Fed him. Gave him a place to sleep. Is that a crime? No. In fact, it's the opposite of being a crime... it's darn right charitable."

"Don't be coy, Bucky. I'm pretty close to taking you downtown for accessory to murder."

I did my best to act shocked. It was the first time he had mentioned the word.

"Murder? What the hell are you talking about, Wilbur?"

"I'm talking about a guy who got his melon cracked open down by Union Square."

"Whoa. You're going too fast. First, you accuse me of theft, and now it's murder? Why not throw in treason and make it a hat trick?"

"You think you're so smart, Bucky, but you've stepped in it this time."

"Whose melon did I supposedly crack?"

"Manny Greenstreet."

"Who's that?"

"The man whose safe you robbed last night."

"I told you, I was here all—"

"Save it. Where's the Swede?"

"What does he have to do with it?"

He stepped back and hitched up his trousers again. Worked his mouth around. He was deliberating on how much information he was going to allow to leak out of his pie hole. "Manny Greenstreet was your boyfriend's new boss. From what I heard, the Swede didn't like the new employment arrangements."

"What? No dental plan?"

"He didn't want to wear a costume and dance around in the ring. So he bashed in Greenstreet's skull."

I gave him an astonished mouth gape. "Not Gus. He's a good kid."

"Yeah, well, that country bumpkin has quite a temper. He went into a rage last night in Greenstreet's office. Tore the place up. I have seven witnesses that will testify to the fact."

"Seven? Wow. That's quite a crowd. Did they charge admission?"

"He also did damage to a couple of wrestlers when they tried to throw him out. Put two of them in the hospital, one with broken ribs and one with a busted jaw. He nearly broke another guy's nose. The guy's a menace to society."

"He sounds it. I'm surprised he didn't pummel me some after eating all my bologna."

"Are you going to tell me where the Swede is or not?"

"I wish I could. We should take someone like that off the street."

"And you too!"

"Me? Don't drag me into it."

"As I said, you're hip-deep. I have an open safe, and a man beaten to death laying on the pavement beneath that opened safe; and I have a known safecracker and a guy with motive having breakfast together. To top it off, I have the corpse's partner having lunch with that same safecracker. Sounds pretty cut and dry."

I said nothing. Hearing it spelled out that way, it looked bad. He stepped back and tugged the handcuffs off his belt again.

"That's it. Turn around, we're going down to the station."

"For what?"

"Aiding and abetting. Obstruction. Breaking and entry. Accessory. Trespassing. Being in the wrong place at the wrong time. You name it."

I stayed quiet. We both knew he didn't have enough to arrest me, but if he wanted to, he could mess up my day pretty good. I was hoping it was a bluff. We stared at each other a bit as he tapped the cuffs against his other hand.

Finally, he said, "Okay, I'm willing to cut a deal with you, Bucky. You say your buddy didn't kill anyone. If that's so, there should be no harm in looking through his suitcase. It might help exonerate him."

"I don't see how."

"Never know 'til we look. Let me take a peek and you avoid a ride downtown. What do you say?"

I didn't like it, but what choice did I have?

25

As a thief, I do have boundaries. When it comes to friends, I avoid poking my nose in where it doesn't belong. I refrain from picking the locks to their apartments. I won't root around in their stuff, break into their safes, or lockers, or pick their pockets, or pry. I'm not naturally nosy. Thief, yes; nosy no.

Currently, Gus was not yet a friend, merely an acquaintance. But I still felt uncomfortable rifling through his personal items. Such morals, however, did not hamper Wilbur. Yet the thing was, I didn't want to spend my day in a holding cell, either.

I stepped back to give a sweep of my hand toward the suitcase in a be-my-guest manner. Crenshaw flashed an eager grin and twisted the case around to face him.

It was a cheap cardboard thing that looked a little worse for wear. Scratches and dings covered it. The clasps were laughable. No locks. As if the manufacturer knew in advance that nothing worth stealing would ever be stowed in such a shoddy product.

Crenshaw clicked the clasps, and the lid popped open like a jack-in-the-box.

I moved behind Crenshaw to peer over his shoulder.

It was packed full.

On top lay a carefully folded satin robe, yellow with white piping. The cuffs and belt were white as well. Wilbur unfolded the garment. Stitched across the back were the words, "Nordstrom the Storming Swede". Done by hand, the lettering was neat and professional-looking nonetheless, and detailed in a way that only a doting mom could accomplish.

"*Storming Swede*," he snorted. "He has a temper like a storm, that's for sure."

He placed the garment on the table. I was grateful that the cat wasn't around to paw at it; he would shred it within minutes.

Sports gear and some street clothes took up much of the space beneath the robe. Jammed into the upper right corner was a set of boxing gloves. Crenshaw pulled them out, and after giving them a cursory look, set them aside.

"So, I take it boxing gloves weren't the murder weapon?" I quipped.

"No. The murder weapon was a piece of furniture, a leg from the desk your boy destroyed."

"Were Gus's prints on this alleged desk leg?"

Crenshaw tightened his lips. He shook his head. "We don't have the hayseed's prints on record and the table leg was wiped clean, anyway. But there were prints on the other pieces of the desk. They've been dusted, and once we get the Swede's prints, I'm sure they'll match."

He was right there. Gus's prints would be all over a good portion of the desk.

Crenshaw turned back to the suitcase and pulled out a pair of leather high-top shoes with smooth soles and long black laces—ring shoes. These he gave a much more careful examination, possibly looking for blood spatter. Finding none, he set them aside, too.

Rummaging inside the case, he found a set of padded headgear, two mouth guards, a pair of punch mitts (for use on speed bags), two pair of boxing trunks (one green and the other yellow), and a coiled jump-rope.

That's when he came across a little item that, in the boxing world, they call the Taylor. He held it up, a question mark in his eyes. I could tell that he couldn't quite make out what it was.

A Taylor has a wide leather band with a pronounced molded strip of shoe leather in the front.

"What's this thing?" he asked. He held it up to his face. "Is it supposed to protect his nose while sparring, or what?"

"It protects the *or what*," I said with a sly grin.

A few years back, Max Schmeling had a heavyweight bout with Jack Sharkey. During the fight, Sharkey got pegged for a controversial, 'low blow' call—he had smacked Schmeling a good one in the...lower regions. They disqualified Sharkey immediately, with Schmeling declared the winner. After that incident, a shoe manufacturer named James P. Taylor started selling an item that he called *Taylor's No Foul Protectors*, specifically designed to protect a fighter's future prospect of spawning a family.

Watching Wilbur hold it up to his face while trying to figure out how to put it on was enjoyable beyond belief.

"That little item," I said, "protects the Swede's Swedish meatballs."

"What are you talking about? Swedish meat..."

Crenshaw dropped Gus's 'item' as if it had become electrified.

"What the hell?" he barked as he rushed to the kitchen sink to scrub his hands.

I laughed so hard I nearly fell over. On principle alone, a man should never fondle another man's Taylor.

Drying his hands with a kitchen towel, Crenshaw returned to the table, his face twisted in a scowl.

"You could've said something sooner," he snapped.

"Hey, I also could've waited until you tried fitting it over your nose."

Ignoring me, he turned his attention to the street clothes in the suitcase, pulling out the trousers and shirt that Gus had been wearing last night when I'd first met him. The pants were scuffed, and a bit torn at the knee. The blood spatters hadn't gone anywhere.

"Well, well, well," muttered Wilbur with satisfaction. "Now we're getting someplace. Blood evidence."

"That happened during the fight with the other wrestlers," I offered.

"Yeah? If I remember right, this morning you told me he'd gotten mugged."

"He did...in a way."

Crenshaw snorted. He checked the pockets of both the pants and the shirt. Nothing. Gus must have emptied the pockets when he changed clothes. He set the garments aside.

The rest of the suitcase contained one clean hound's-tooth polo shirt, but no other slacks. Crenshaw checked the pocket of the shirt, too. Nothing. A small toilet kit was there. Crenshaw opened the zipper and took a peek. His fingers moved things around inside the pouch; however, he either found nothing of interest, or he was loath to touch any more of Gus's personal items because he quickly zipped the pouch back up.

The upper lid of the case had a sleeve sewn across the face; tucked inside were several sets of underwear: boxers and sleeveless undershirts. He left those untouched, too.

Then he came across an over-sized leather billfold jammed into the sleeve. Opening it, his eyes widened.

"What's this?" he asked triumphantly. "Why, it's a calling card for Manford Greenstreet—our victim."

"So what?" I asked.

"So, it can help place him at the scene."

"I thought seven witnesses already did that?"

He snorted and continued his exploration of the billfold. He found a few receipts and a couple of ticket stubs from Gus's journey to the big city: a bus ticket from Minneapolis to Chicago, and the train ticket stub from Chicago to New York. I breathed a sigh of relief when I noticed the train ticket was for the Lake Shore Limited and that it had arrived four days ago, just like Gus had told me.

Crenshaw must have thought the ticket stubs to be inconsequential, for he set them aside without a second look.

That's when he pulled an item from the billfold that caused my throat to constrict.

It came in the form of a folded two-page document. When Crenshaw opened it, his gnomish face became radiant.

"Ah," he said. "I've just discovered motive."

———◦———

26

It was Gus's copy of the contract that he'd signed with The Knicker-bocker Wrestling Federation.

Glancing over Wilbur's shoulder, I tried skimming the document. It was full of legalese doublespeak that locked Gus into a lifetime of cuddling with sweaty men inside the ropes of a wrestling ring. At the bottom of page two were the signatures needed to close the deal: Gustave Nordstrom and Manford Greenstreet. Lock, stock, and barrel.

"That just about sums it up," gloated Crenshaw. "We have motive, opportunity, and the means."

"C'mon, Wilbur," I cried, "Gus isn't a killer. You think this piece of paper goes to motive?"

"Sure. Greenstreet signed him up for a lifetime membership to his wrestling puppet show. My witnesses say that the Swede felt scammed, wasn't happy about it."

"Did those witnesses see him kill the guy?"

"No, but—"

"And when was his opportunity? What time did Greenstreet get his ticket punched?"

"The coroner puts it between one and three in the morning."

"Then it couldn't have been Gus. He was with me at that time."

"So you say. But I'm still looking to you for opening that safe, and that makes the two of you each other's alibis, doesn't it? Pretty convenient."

"Listen, my alibi is solid. I was at The Famous Door. I left at midnight and met—"

"Yeah, yeah. I checked with Socks down at the club. He backs your story about the time frame for when you left there. But that doesn't clear you. Union Square is only twenty minutes away. That gives you plenty of time to meet up with hayseed and together go pay dear Manny a visit. And while you're opening the safe, your friend is going ape on Greenstreet's noggin."

"Yeah, like that makes sense. The two of us, having just met for the first time, decide to go into a life of crime together."

"Who says you just met? You two could've known each other for years."

"The kid's only been in town for four days—you saw the ticket stubs in the billfold."

"Okay, so you've known each other for a few days, then. Plenty of time to plan this out."

"You told me there were no fingerprints on the murder weapon. How about on the safe? Any prints there?"

"You mean the one you opened? You and I both know that you're too smart to leave prints at a crime scene."

"What was taken from the safe?"

"You tell me."

"C'mon, Wilbur. At least tell me what I took from it. Maybe I'll go root around in my cupboards and see if it matches my hidden contraband."

"You took all of last night's gate for their wrestling show—around four grand."

I raised my eyebrows. "Wow! I wish I did know how to crack safes. That's pretty good money. Was anything else taken?"

He shrugged. "Some legal matters—papers and stuff."

"And why would I have any interest in taking Greenstreet's legal matters?"

"Just to clean him out real good." He leaned in, a glint in his eye. "Oh...you also stole a .32 automatic that was in the safe."

I recoiled at that. I hadn't thought about a gun being locked away. He turned to peer around the apartment. "Would I find that .32 automatic in your contraband closet if I got a warrant?" he asked.

"My first response is no," I said, "but who knows what you cops could drop on me."

Crenshaw frowned. He looked hurt. "You know I don't play that way, Bucky."

"That's a pretty detailed list for an empty safe, Wilbur. How do you know about the stuff that was taken? I'm sure Manny Greenstreet didn't tell you about it, him being dead and all."

"Greenstreet's business partner filled us in—you know, the fella you were eating lunch with."

"Big Bob Barton?"

"No, the other guy—the one I had just got done questioning an hour earlier."

Playing like I was hearing fresh information, I said: "Oh, that other guy in the booth was Greenstreet's partner? What's his name?"

"Mickey Jacobs."

"The famous fight promoter?"

"No, you idiot, that's Mike Jacobs. Greenstreet's partner is *Mickey* Jacobs."

"Sounds confusing. Does this Mickey character know the combination to the safe?"

"Sure, but he has an alibi. He was doing some wrestling of his own at the time."

"There was another wrestling show after midnight?"

A leer formed on Crenshaw's face. "Naw, this was the other kind of wrestling—the happy kind. He was at his apartment all night with another wrestler."

I raised an eyebrow.

"Not like that! It's a girl wrestler by the name of Flo Hitchcock. She used to be a burlesque dancer, now she dresses up like a nurse and wrestles under the name, Florence Fighting-gale—if you can believe it."

I could, and did. I was now convinced that the pretty woman at Woolworth's was Florence Fighting-gale—the same nurse that Gus spoke about being in Greenstreet's office when he had his little temper tantrum. But, it also made me wonder, did a female wrestler have the capacity to swing a desk leg with enough oomph to bash in a skull? Probably.

"Have you considered the two of them?" I asked. "They could have done it together."

"Jacobs and Nurse Flo?"

"Sure, why not?"

He shook his head.

"The doorman at Jacob's building confirms that the two lovebirds came through the lobby around midnight and went straight upstairs...and didn't come back down until morning."

"Still, there could be a back door to the—"

"There's no back door." He let out a sigh of exasperation. "Look, the safe in Greenstreet's office contained gate proceeds and some legal matters connected to their partnership—contracts and things like that. Why would Mickey Jacobs rob his own safe?"

"To make it look like someone else had broken in. I imagine that with Manny Greenstreet out of the picture, the entire wrestling business falls into Mickey Jacob's lap."

He hesitated. I caught his lips pinching. He glanced away.

"Wait a minute," I blurted. "Jacobs *doesn't* get Greenstreet's half, does he? Someone else is in the picture. Who?"

Of course, this afternoon, I had already learned about the 'turf-war' between Jacobs and Greenstreet, and how Jacobs wanted to sell their puny operation to Big Bob Barton's wrestling outfit, but I wasn't about to tell Wilbur that—at least not yet.

But there was something else to this. I could see him equivocating. He knew something that I didn't.

"Is it Big Bob Barton?" I asked. "Is he the other partner?"

"No," he muttered. "There is no other partner...at least, there wasn't until Greenstreet got croaked."

"Let me guess, his half goes to another party in the course of his demise."

He gave a curt nod.

"Who?"

"Someone we're not realistically looking at."

"Why not?"

"Because it's just not feasible."

"Is this person tied to Mickey Jacobs?"

He snorted with exasperation. "Look, at first I thought Mickey Jacobs was the perfect suspect, too. From what I heard, he and Greenstreet may have been partners, but they didn't get along very well. That's why I spent so much time questioning Jacobs this morning—and why I put a tail on him when I got done with him. He had the perfect motive for wanting Greenstreet dead. That's also why I checked on his whereabouts for the time of the murder. But like I told you, he was nowhere near the Knickerbocker Club from eleven fifteen on. He couldn't have done it. Flo Hitchcock—a.k.a. Florence Fighting-gale—swears he was with her all night and they never left the apartment."

"He could have hired someone to do it." I offered.

"Maybe. But, again, why steal his own money? And besides, when I questioned him, he was shaken up about it. Pretty authentic. I don't think it was him."

"How about this Barton character? Does he have a motive for wanting Manny dead?"

"We looked at him. Jacobs told us he and Greenstreet were in talks about selling their operation to him. So I sent one of my guys over to Big Bob's office to interview him this morning. His alibi checked out, too. He was at a club downtown. At least ten other people can account for him at the time of Greenstreet's demise."

"That's a pretty good alibi," I said. "Maybe too good."

"It checks out," said Crenshaw adamantly.

"You told me he's connected to the mob. It could've been a hit. He could've had it done."

"It wasn't a hit. From everything we know, Greenstreet was just about to sell his operation to Barton. They were in negotiations. Why would Barton kill him?"

"Wait. Greenstreet wanted to sell the wrestling club to Barton?" That wasn't what Nick Terrano had told me. He'd said that Greenstreet was resistant to the idea. Had Nick got it wrong?

My thoughts went to the Chicago angle and the snippets of information that I'd gleaned throughout the day concerning the Italian mob. They had an interest in buying the wrestling club, too. I desperately wanted to bring up the subject, but didn't know how to do it without getting myself into deeper trouble.

"Well, someone benefits from Greenstreet's demise," I said. "Who gets his part of the show now?"

Crenshaw drew in a heavy sigh, as if reluctant to share, but he finally relented. "Greenstreet's sister."

"Sister?"

"Yeah, his sister, okay?"

"What's her name?"

"Velma Bomberg."

27

BOMBERG.

I gave a start.

The name Bomberg struck a chord. An hour ago, it had tumbled out of Big Bob Barton's ugly lips. What had Barton said? Oh, right:

I know that Bomberg talked to the wops in Chicago. But Bomberg knows the score.

Had he been referring to Greenstreet's sister? That didn't feel right. I had gotten the impression that Barton thought of Bomberg as some sort of threat—and that Bomberg might have connections to the Italian mob. Did she? Or was she connected to the Jewish mob here in New York?

During our little slapping session at lunch, he also thought that I knew Bomberg personally and that possibly I had been sent here from Chicago. He'd warned that Bomberg shouldn't be attempting a double-cross. But what kind of double-cross did he mean?

Could Velma Bomberg be the brains behind the whole operation? The negotiator? The puppet master? Was she involved in her own brother's murder?

"So this sister, Velma, gets her brother's stake in the wrestling show?" I asked, suddenly interested in this alternative possibility.

"That's right."

"All of it?"

"I said so, didn't I?"

"What was her relationship like with her brother?"

He shrugged. "They had their differences, squabbled some, but...you know, they were family."

"Could she have killed him?"

He chortled. "Mrs. Bomberg? You haven't met her, have you?"

I just stared at him.

"I'd be surprised if she weighs a hundred pounds. Sure, she's a mean old goat—she doesn't care for cops, that's for sure—but I can't picture her swinging a table leg with enough force to bash in a human skull."

"But you talked to her?"

"Yeah, we talked to her. We had to tell her about her brother. Greenstreet wasn't married, and she was next of kin."

"And she has an alibi?"

He hesitated. "Well, no. Not exactly."

"Where was she at the time of the murder?" I asked.

"Sleeping."

"Alone?"

"Yeah, alone. Her husband was out of town."

"So she can't account for her whereabouts."

"You're grabbing at straws, Bucky. The woman didn't kill her brother."

"What about her husband?"

"What about him?"

"Could he have done it?"

"Are your ears on the blink? I just told you, he was out of town...on business."

"And you know that for sure? Maybe it's a ruse."

"Yes, I know that for sure! He was traveling. He didn't get into town until this morning."

"You checked him out?"

"Yes, I checked him out. Talked to him just before lunch. His alibi is good."

Blast. It seemed every suspect anywhere near this thing had a solid alibi.

Except for Mrs. Bomberg, that is. And from Crenshaw's description, she couldn't swing a broom, let alone a desk leg.

"Look," said Crenshaw, "I know you're trying to deflect suspicion away from your buddy, but it would be in your best interest—as well as his—for you to just tell me where he is."

I tightened my lips.

"We have your boy's description out on the wires. We're gonna pick him up, eventually. It would be better if he came in on his own. We just want to talk to him."

He began replacing the items back into the suitcase.

"If it's like you say, and the Swede didn't kill Greenstreet, then he has nothing to fear."

I hesitated, staring at him. I couldn't give up Gus. Not yet. Not until I figured this out.

"Bucky, I only want the truth. If he's innocent, then we can clear him, and he can go back to wrestling, or boxing, or whatever other sport he wants." He held up the set of boxing gloves. "Then he won't have to carry all this crap around town in a suitcase. He can stow it in a gym locker somewhere, like down at..."

He halted in mid-sentence. He blinked twice. I could almost smell the cams and gears in his 'brain box' chugging out a notion.

"He's not a wrestler, he's a boxer..." he muttered half to himself, half to me.

Of course, I'd been trying to tell him that all along, but to say so now would only oil up the cams and gears, and I could see where he was going with his notion.

A crafty smile oozed into his dopey mug. He stepped back. The notion fully engaged. And I didn't care for the direction it had taken. He suddenly looked smug.

He pointed his finger gun at me. "You stay put, Bucky. Don't leave the apartment. I'm gonna have some more questions for you in an hour or two."

"Leaving so soon?" I tamped down the alarm exploding in my thoughts.

The grin was full wattage now. "Yeah. I've got some business to take care of. But I'm coming back, you can count on it."

He glanced over at Gus's suitcase.

"And when I do, I'll have a warrant this time. You touch anything or go anyplace, I'll have you in jail before nightfall!"

Wilbur couldn't get to the door fast enough.

He knew. I could see it. Crenshaw was aware of my relationship with Nick Terrano—and Pop's relationship with him as well. He had connected the dots.

He was headed to the gym to pick up Gus.

28

I EASED UP TO the front bay window to watch for Crenshaw leaving the building on the street below. He soon appeared, arms swinging jubilantly as he rushed to his unmarked cruiser. He glanced up before getting into the car. He fired his finger gun at me again, warning me to stay put. The full-wattage smile blazing.

That's okay, take a picture, Wilbur. I want you to see me still in the apartment.

He climbed into the cruiser and screeched away.

Immediately, I turned and bolted through the door. I needed to get to the telephone on the second-floor landing right away. I had to warn Nick that Crenshaw was coming. He needed to hide Gus some place fast.

However, as I came bounding down the stairs and onto the second-floor landing, I came to a screeching halt.

Mrs. Bernstein stood there with the ear-cone up to her ear, her lips kissing the mouthpiece on the wall. Blabbing away. Blabbing away.

Smack in the middle of a sordid tale of love and betrayal, her face was flushed with the excitement of red-meat gossip.

"I wouldn't put it past Martha if she left the cheating scoundrel. It would be his just desserts if his secretary grew fat and disgusting. Of course, that kind of thing could never happen to my Floyd, because I take care of myself. *And* I keep Floyd happy in the...well, you know. And a happy husband never has to..." Blah, blah, blah.

For five full minutes I stood there, glaring impatiently while the juices in my stomach roiled. Mrs. Bernstein shot disapproving glances at me, as if annoyed by the impertinence of my listening in on her lurid conversation.

After what seemed like forever, she covered the mouthpiece with her hand and bared her teeth at me. She had no intention of hanging up anytime soon. She was in the middle of a full gossip blitz.

Exasperated, I turned and barreled down the stairs to the street and jogged down the block and around the corner to the Rexall drugstore. I knew they had a telephone booth in the back. I dodged around customers and whipped past the shelves to where the booth sat.

And wouldn't you know!...it was occupied.

I stood outside the booth, pacing and glancing at my watch for several minutes before the doors folded open and a man stepped out. He grinned at me.

"Sorry it took so long," he said. "I—"

I pushed past him in a huff of rudeness and slid into the booth, closing the door in his face. I pressed a nickel into the slot and got the operator on the line, giving her the number for Nick's gym. It rang nonstop for twelve rings.

The operator broke in to tell me the obvious: "There is no answer, sir, would you—"

"Let it ring!" I yelled. It continued to do so.

A decade ticked by. No one was there.

I hung up.

Once the nickel spit out, I shoved it back into the slot and got another operator. I gave her Nick's home phone number.

His wife, Angelica, answered after three rings. "Hello, Mrs. Terrano, this is—"

"Buck Flynn, is that you? How are you, young man?" she asked. "We haven't seen you for ages."

"I'm fine. Could I speak to Nick, please Mrs. Terrano?"

"We were all just sitting around the table talking about you, Buck," she said. "That nice boy, Gustave Nordstrom, is here. What a treasure. A good wholesome boy."

"Yes, he's a great kid. Is Nick in?"

"Gus is so courteous. He pulls out the chair for me and the girls—treats us like ladies. He says, 'yes sir' and 'yes ma'am'—just like a gentleman."

"That's Gus, listen I—"

"That's the sign of good upbringing, you know."

"Yes, I suppose it is."

"His parents should be proud of him."

"I'm sure they are."

"Francesca and Regina are hanging on his every word. He told us how you took him in and helped him out. You are such a sweet boy helping him out that way. Both of you are such nice boys."

"Thank-you, Mrs. Terrano. Could I—"

Her voice became a whisper. "Francesca and Regina think Gus is very good looking. So handsome, with that frock of blond hair and his blue eyes. And so big. He looks as strong as an ox."

"Yes, I suppose he is, but—"

"Nicolas told me he's a boxer, too. Isn't that nice? Such a coincidence, don't you think. Although, it's hard to picture such a nice boy like that being a boxer. But I'm told he's quite an excellent boxer."

"I—"

"Why, I just had a thought, Buck. You should come over tonight. Join us for dinner. We haven't eaten yet. There's plenty to go around. We're having chicken cacciatore and I have leftover penne all'arrabbiata that I can heat up. We can open a bottle of Chianti and—"

"That sounds delicious, but—"

"All of us can talk and get to know Gus better. I'm sure that Francesca and Regina would be thrilled to see you, Buck. They love having you around. Especially Gina. She speaks of you often. She really...Oh my! I just had another thought. Wouldn't it be nice if you and Gustave took

Francesca and Regina out tonight? Maybe to a moving picture show. Show the girls the town."

"I don't think tonight works, I've—"

"The four of you together. I can just picture it. Gus and Francesca, you and Regina, you would make such handsome couples. Yes. I think that would be nice."

"Mrs. Terrano, could you please put Nick on the phone?"

And seven minutes later, she did just that.

"Crenshaw is on his way to your place," I blurted once Nick came on the line.

"Here? At my house? I don't like the sound of that."

"Look, he left my apartment in a huff. I'm pretty sure he's headed for the gym first. But when he finds it closed, I wouldn't put it past him to come knocking on your door."

Nick let loose a low-grade growl. "What will the neighbors think? The police coming here? No. I don't like that a bit."

"I'm sorry, Nick. There was nothing I could do. Crenshaw just put two and two together and—"

"I would hate to see Gus get arrested in front of the girls."

"I would hate to see Gus get arrested, period."

"I'll get him out of here."

"You better do it quick. It took a while to get a hold of you."

"Yeah, thanks for the heads up."

I was about to hang up when a thought came to me. "Hey Nick, this afternoon when you told me about the turf war between Manny Greenstreet and Mickey Jacobs, you said that Jacobs wanted to sell to Big Bob Barton, but Manny didn't...right?"

Dead air seeped through the phone. I waited.

"Is that what I said?"

"Yes, that's what you told me, remember?"

"I suppose."

"Could it have been the other way around? Could it have been Jacobs who didn't want to sell?"

"I don't think so. My guy said it was Greenstreet who was exploring other options. I told you, he even went out to Chicago to look for franchise opportunities."

Chicago. The Italian mob.

"How reliable is your guy?" I asked.

"Pretty solid, he's a lawyer that I've dealt with. He got it straight from Greenstreet's lawyer's mouth. Apparently, they belong to the same club downtown. Oh! That reminds me. You wanted the name and address of Manny Greenstreet's lawyer. You still want that information?"

"You have it?"

"Yeah. Let me find it."

I didn't see how it could help me now, but if nothing else panned out, I could use it as a last resort. I heard him on the other end of the line, fumbling around in his pockets.

"I got it here somewhere..."

As I waited, I noticed a pencil dangling on a string next to the telephone. I opened the phone book lying there and found an edge to scribble down the address. Nick came back on the line.

"Okay, his office is at 401..."

As the street address came squawking over the telephone wire, I paused in mid scribble, dumbfounded.

"Wait, Nick!" I said. "Are you sure this is the right address for the lawyer?"

"It's the address my friend gave me."

"But this is the street address of the wrestling club."

"What wrestling club?"

"The Knickerbocker Club—Greenstreet's outfit."

"Oh, is it? I hadn't noticed, but yeah, I guess that's where his office is."

"I find that strange."

"Hmm...I don't see why."

"Because Gus told me Greenstreet had intended to run the signed contract up to his lawyer's office...you know uptown."

"Did Gus say it was uptown?"

It suddenly dawned on me that maybe he hadn't. "Ask him."

I waited, listening to a brief but muffled conversation. Nick came back on the line.

"He knows nothing about a lawyer uptown. He doesn't even know which direction uptown is. Greenstreet just told him he was going to run it up to his lawyer first thing in the morning."

Then it hit me. Greenstreet didn't mean uptown at all. He literally meant up—as to the fourth floor of the same building: suite 401.

"What's the lawyer's name?" I asked.

"Bomberg, Bernard Bomberg."

I nearly dropped my pencil. "The lawyer's name is Bomberg?"

"Yeah, that's right, Bernard. But I was told that everyone calls him Bernie."

"Greenstreet's sister has the last name of Bomberg too."

"Does she? Hmm...maybe they're related."

"Husband and wife," I muttered. "Bernie Bomberg is Greenstreet's brother-in-law."

"I suppose. My guy said nothing about it."

"So Greenstreet's brother-in-law has an office on the fourth floor above the club?"

"It looks like it."

Suddenly, aspects of this whole affair aligned in my mind. Things beginning to fit.

I was about to ask Nick another question when he blurted:

"Uh-oh. Someone's knocking at the door..."

"Don't answer it, Nick," I yelled.

"Don't answer the door, Angelica!" I heard him yell.

Pause. I had a death grip on the phone's ear-cone. Over the receiver, I heard muffled voices.

"Damn...it's too late, Buck," said Nick. "Angie just let Crenshaw in."

Suddenly, I heard nothing but dead air.

———◆○◆———

29

I STOOD IN THE phone booth, somewhat shell-shocked.

At this moment, Gus was being arrested. And there was nothing I could do about it.

Not only that. A bombshell had just dropped.

Greenstreet's lawyer was his brother-in-law, too. What did it mean? Well, for one thing, it meant that the control of Manny's half of The Knickerbocker Wrestling Federation stayed in the family—sort of.

I glanced down at the phone book and the address that I had begun to scribble down on the page edge. I didn't need it now. I already knew how to get to the wrestling club—I'd been there twice in the last sixteen hours. So I closed up the book.

I slid open the door to exit the booth, but stopped short.

A thought crawled over my cranium. A time-line formulated. And it involved snippets of information that I'd gleaned throughout the day; from overheard conversations to slapping sessions at lunch; from alibis and train schedules to double-crosses. And to top it off...two competing mob interests.

But the time-line crystalizing in my head also involved my disastrous visit to the wrestling club last night. Something I had overlooked. Something I had seen, yet hadn't seen.

Until now.

Turning around, I swept up the phone book again and flipped through its pages. I found what I was looking for: Name. Phone. And address. I memorized it. I looked up another name. Found it: Name. Phone. Address. I memorized that too.

I left the phone booth and rushed back up to my apartment.

Coming through the apartment door, I heard the squeaky pawing of the cat outside the kitchen window. I ignored him and hurried over to the kitchen drawer to grab my screwdriver. The beast spotted me through the glass and the squeaks increased with a feverish tenacity, as if attempting to sway me by sheer determination.

Sorry, Kittens. No time for you tonight. But I got a new name to call you today: Bomberg! Don't like it? Too bad.

I bent down to unscrew the grate to the air return shaft, reached up into the hole, grabbed my tools from inside, and screwed the grate back in place.

I had little time. Crenshaw would be looking for me. Sooner than later, he would burst into my apartment with that search warrant, and I didn't want to be here when he arrived—my tools either. He would find them for sure, and I couldn't lose the only inheritance Pops had left me.

Gus was probably already in custody—either in the backseat of Crenshaw's car, or already downtown being processed and heading to a holding cell. Either way, there was nothing I could do about that, but I had an idea that just might get us both out of this jam.

And maybe bring a killer to light, too.

I only hoped Gus had the good sense to keep his trap shut about me going to Union Square last night. If he spilled the beans about that, Crenshaw would arrest me, for sure. Maybe not for murder, and not even for theft, but definitely for breaking and entry.

Any charge worthy enough to become a notch on Crenshaw's service weapon.

In the bedroom, I changed into my 'work clothes'—everything except my skullcap and the pair of Dent's gloves. I slipped those items into the pockets of a topcoat, which I slipped on over my uniform.

I grabbed my black fedora and left the apartment

And yes, I was wearing my crepe-soled shoes.

———◈———

30

Now that I was out of the apartment, I had time to kill. It was still early evening, and there was nothing I could accomplish until after hours, so in the meantime, I decided to check into a hotel. That would at least get me off the street for the time being...and would also help me with a very important personal need: sleep.

Because of last night's escapade, I was cooking on about two hours of nocturnal fuel. My tank was running on vapors. There was a good possibility that I would make three separate 'unannounced' visits tonight, maybe more, and I needed to be sharp. A nap was in order.

However, before checking into a hotel, I had two chores to accomplish. The first was to make a stop at Heymann's butcher shop on Sixth Avenue.

I went in and made my purchase. They wrapped it up nicely for me, and I left the shop to find a telephone booth out on the street. My second chore was to call Nick Terrano to check on Gus's status.

I found a booth on the corner. Pressing a nickel into the slot, I got an operator and called Nick's house. The phone rang for several minutes. It didn't sound like anyone was home, which worried me some. I was about to hang up when a female voice burst on the line, warbling and wheezing with intermittent sobs. It was one of Nick's daughters. It took a while to discover, but it ended up being Francesca.

"Gone!" she wailed. "Gus is gone. Some policeman came and got him."

I could almost feel snot seeping through the receiver.

"Is your dad there?" I asked between wails.

"No!" she yelled. "He and mother followed the police car to the jail—to jail, Buck! Gus is in jail."

"Yeah, I got that."

"What am I ever going to do now?" she cried.

She was coming off like a bride whose groom had just croaked. Geeze, she'd just met the fellow a couple of hours ago.

"We go on living, I suppose," I offered.

"But, it's Gus, Buck. Gus! He had so much potential."

"Maybe you should go be with your sister," I said. Never having had a sister myself, this explosion of emotions was unfamiliar territory for me.

"Gina?" she moaned. "I can't be around her right now. She's too emotional. Just a mess. She doesn't have my strength. She doesn't know how to hold it together."

Whoa! This was holding it together? She fussed for a few minutes more, but I couldn't handle it. I finally had to hang up before the poor thing slit her wrists.

That sealed it. Gus was in custody. That meant it was up to me. I only hoped my planned activities for tonight could turn things around.

I left the phone booth and walked a few blocks, heading toward Union Square. I found a cheap hotel and paid cash for a room for one night. And trudged up the stairs to it. I did my best to push aside all the thoughts colliding in my brain. It had been a long day, and I needed to calm my mind and rest my body.

I took off my topcoat and hat and laid down on the bed fully clothed.

And for five hours...blessed sleep.

I awoke to darkness filling the room. I felt somewhat rested, but a bit foggy. I went down the hall to the bathroom. The rest of the hotel was asleep. I stripped down and took a shower. The water never got hot, but that was okay; the cold water revived me.

I re-dressed into my 'work clothes', slipped into my topcoat and hat, and set out. Hopefully, to uncover a murderer.

31

THE LOBBY WAS EMPTY when I left the hotel, not even a desk clerk in sight.

I walked to Union Square right past S. Kleins Department Store and past my old buddy Lafayette. Coming up the block, I approached the Knickerbocker Wrestling Federation.

The street was empty.

For ten minutes, I stood in the doorway of the abandoned building across the way, watching. Behind me, I noticed that the chain on the door still dangled; the lock undone from earlier today. I closed things up—just in case Detective Crenshaw followed up on that, too.

Nothing stirred in the street or in the building across from me. I spent most of the time scrutinizing a specific window on the fourth floor. The light was on, just like it had been last night. But then I expected it to be.

If I was right, no one had been in or out of that particular office all day. At least, I hoped not.

Bernard Bomberg's office.

It all made sense now.

The whole reason I'd broken into Manny Greenstreet's office in the first place was because Gus had told me Manny still had Gus's signed contract—supposedly locked in the safe. Manny told him he was holding it until his lawyer got back from Chicago, and would 'run it up' to his office first thing in the morning. Yes, literally *up*—as in up to the fourth floor.

Earlier, after talking with Detective Crenshaw—and Nick as well—I remembered some things that helped me piece together a working time-line for Manny Greenstreet's murder. I based part of that timeline on information that only I knew, and the cops didn't. And if my time-line was right, only one person could have killed Manny.

There were still holes in my theory, but I was about to fill a couple of those holes right now.

However, even if my theory proved correct, I still faced a major problem.

Somehow, I had to get the specific information—that only I knew—into the hands of the police without implicating myself. If I openly told them everything I knew, Crenshaw would certainly arrest me. Maybe not for murder, but at least for breaking and entry. I needed to point them in the right direction without confessing to being at the crime scene last night.

Could it be done?

Time to find out.

I crossed the street and let myself into the building.

The main lobby was as dark and quiet as an empty casket. The hallway that led to the Knickerbocker Club in the back hadn't moved. Neither had the elevator. But I didn't bother with either of them. I headed for the stairs instead, silently skipping up four flights. I rarely use an elevator during an after-hours visit. No matter how modern or quiet an elevator is, the noise of it—even the 'ding' at the end of the ride—echoes throughout a dark building. Plus, you never know what to expect when doors open.

Room 401 was to the right of the staircase, placing the office at the front of the building. Stenciled on the frosted glass of the door was the name Bernard Bomberg, Attorney at Law.

I took out my packet of lock-picks and let myself into the office, closing the door behind me. The lights blazed. Normally, such brightness makes me uncomfortable. But someone else had left the lights on, so I wasn't about to turn them off.

The office was much neater than Greenstreet's office had been last night, and the desk was upright and intact. Obviously, *The Storming Swede* hadn't paid a visit yet.

It didn't take long to find what I had expected to find.

A safe.

I found it hidden behind an oil painting on the wall. It was the same make and model installed in Greenstreet's office below: a Meilink, Hercules. And as I've already mentioned, it's a safe designed to be more fireproof than burglar-proof. And that makes me happy.

I tugged my right-hand glove off a finger at a time. The Dents are thin, but not thin enough for what I was about to do. This would be the only time of the evening that I would be gloveless.

I was about to twirl the dial to clear the wheels...when I paused. Recalling my experience from last night, I had heeded one of Pop's obscure rules, and it had saved me a boatload of time—even if it had brought a boatload of trouble, too.

> *"Always give a tug first. A lot of idiots own safes. And idiots sometimes forget to twirl the dial when locking up."*

Could I get lucky a second time? After all, according to my theory, it was probably the same 'idiot' that had closed the safe downstairs last night...and he hadn't twirled the dial then.

Grabbing the handle, I twisted it.

Nope. Rock-solid.

Oh well. It was worth a try. Not to fret. It would not be sealed for long.

———◆———

32

CRACKING A SAFE BEGINS with an understanding of how a combination lock works.

Behind each dial is a spindle with a drive cam on the far end. Surrounding the spindle are wheels, tumblers, one for each number in the combination: three wheels, three numbers; four wheels, four numbers, and so on. The more wheels, the harder it is to discover the combination. I already knew that this Meilink model had three wheels, so I didn't need to waste time figuring that out.

Each wheel has a gate, or notch, cut into its outer edge. These gates need to align perfectly. The moment they do, a metal rod, called a fence, drops into the notches. The fence controls the locking mechanism itself, and once it's in place, the lock is breached and the door can open.

But before that can happen, I needed to find the contact area of the drive cam. Just like the wheels, the cam is notched, a sloped notch meant to catch the lever. This is an important first step to discovering the rest of the notches in the wheels on the spindle.

I closed my eyes and took a deep, cleansing breath. I let the silence solidify around me. Discovering the contact area of a drive cam happens with a faint double click. Very faint.

Normally, I use a stethoscope to crack a safe. It makes the job much easier. But unfortunately, it was in my locker at Penn Station. Not knowing the model of the safe beforehand, I had debated whether to swing by and pick it up but had chosen not to for time's sake. The Hercules wouldn't be a problem, however. It was so cheaply made that Benny Goodman could be playing in the next room and I could still hear the clicks.

I twirled the dial around a few times to clear the wheels. Pressing an ear against the cold steel of the safe door, I listened to the deadness inside. I mentally extended my senses into the nerve endings of my fingertips.

Let the delicate work begin.

After a few minutes, I clearly heard the double click I was listening for. I'd found the contact area on the dial. The next order of business was to—what they call in the business—park the wheels. By setting the combination dial directly opposite the contact area. From there, I began decoding the combination by listening intently for the ensuing clicks of the wheels. It becomes a process of elimination at this point, throwing away dead numbers and holding the true ones. The tricky part is keeping track of the variations in my head. Normally, it's best to use a pencil and paper at this phase, to give order to the process and not duplicate yourself, but I enjoy the mental challenge of it. I was raised twisting dials like this and it's nearly second nature to me.

Twenty minutes later, the gate aligned, and I heard that wonderful hushed click as the fence fell into place.

The safe was breached.

First things first.

I immediately retrieved a small square chamois from my jacket pocket and wiped the dial clean of prints. I then put my right-hand glove back on—a caution I am fastidious about—and only then did I open the safe.

Hoping to find more than emptiness this time.

———◦———

33

PACKED. AS EXPECTED.

Inside were several stacks of papers and files. But two other items tucked inside the safe drew my attention immediately.

The first was a large leather pouch—a bank bag. The presence of bank bags always gets my blood churning. Nine times out of ten, they contain cash. This pouch was crammed in next to the files. I pulled it out to look it over. It felt heavy. It had a zipper along the top. Sometimes these types of bags also have a cute little lock attached—cute enough to open in about seven seconds—but this one didn't. I unzipped it, letting out a soft whistle as I did.

Cash was jammed into it. Had to be thirty or forty thousand dollars. The mother lode.

My first inclination, of course—being a thief—was to take the money and run. After all, that's a lot of green. However, I also knew that I was here for a greater purpose, and that purpose was to clear Gus and me of potential murder charges. That meant making sure all the evidence pointed to the actual killer and not to us. This money could very well be such evidence.

Taking the cash was out of the question, it would only bring undue attention. And on top of that, I was pretty sure that this was the same bank bag taken from Greenstreet's safe last night—to make it look like a robbery gone bad.

However, if that was the case, another question came into play. Why so much money?

Crenshaw had mentioned that the gate from last night's wrestling show had been stolen. He had even told me the amount: 'just over four grand' he'd said. But there was nearly ten times that here.

Then it dawned on me. The rest of the money had to do with business—nasty business.

Someone had divided the money into two distinct bundles. A small wad of about five thousand dollars was rubber-banded together, and the other was a larger wad, made up of stacks of newer bills banded with paper—the way fresh money comes from a bank. Those stacks were also rubber-banded together as a complete unit.

Just the way a payoff might be distributed.

The larger wad of money had to be one of two things: illicit gains, or a cash down payment of some kind.

That kind of cash presents quite a temptation, but I needed to leave it alone.

However...

Last night I had gone to Greenstreet's office with two goals in mind: to find Gus's contract and, if possible, re-coup the money that Greenstreet had swindled from him. Since there was more than enough to account for last night's gate in the bag, I decided to at least re-pay Gus the money he had lost. From the smaller stack, I counted out two hundred and sixty dollars and put it in one of my pockets. Gus's refund exactly.

I zipped up the bag and—with all the willpower I could muster—returned it to the safe.

The second item inside the safe—which had stood out when I'd first opened it—confirmed to me that the bank bag was, in fact, the one which had been stolen from Greenstreet's safe. How did I know? Because Crenshaw had mentioned another item taken from the safe: a handgun.

An Iver Johnson Hammerless .32 Automatic was lying on top of the stack of files.

Was it the one stolen from Greenstreet's safe? I would make book on it. Crenshaw told me the stolen gun had been a .32.

I moved the handgun over on top of the bank-bag so I could with-draw the stack of files. I turned and carried the stack over to Bomberg's desk—thankfully, without tripping over a body this time. Setting the files down, I moved his candlestick telephone over to one side, clearing a spot. I took a seat and began finger-walking through the stack.

I came across Gus's contract right away. Because of the murder down-stairs and yesterday's police presence, the document had yet to be officially filed. Bernie Bomberg didn't want to be anywhere near his office. He had avoided it like the plague all day yesterday.

I didn't take the time to read the two-page document, but it looked ex-actly like the one Crenshaw had discovered in Gus's suitcase. His signature was at the bottom of page two, right next to Manford Greenstreet's scrawl.

I folded it up and tucked it into my jacket pocket.

It had taken twenty-four hours—and for Gus, a trip to a holding cell—but at least that task had been accomplished. I began re-stacking the files when my eyes fell across another document lying on top. And the title made me curious:

Merger and Acquisition Title Form.

I scanned it briefly. The mass of words on the document was an ocean of legalese, making my head swim, but I caught the gist of the document and the principals involved. From what I could make out, it looked to be a major stake acquisition of The Knickerbocker Wrestling Federation by some corporate interest in Chicago. The dollar numbers involved were as-tronomical—nearly two hundred thousand dollars, with a cash down-pay-ment of...yep, forty thousand dollars—the same amount bundled together there in the safe.

I thought back to my slapping session with Big Bob Barton. What had he said?

"Bomberg knows the score...if he's planning a double-cross to throw in with the wops, he's gonna be sorry..."

It looked like Bomberg had planned a double-cross all along. He was throwing in with the Italian mob alright.

The question is, did he do it with, or without, Manny Greenstreet's blessing. If it was without his blessing, and it involved that kind of cash, I could easily see it leading to murder.

Turning to the back pages, it stunned me to find that the document had already been signed and notarized. Then I recalled the conversation that I'd overheard in the abandoned building.

Gravelly-voice had asked about the documents. He wanted to take them back with him. Asked if they had already been signed. The other fellow told him they had.

It was a done deal! Sort of.

As my eyes fell to the bottom of the page, I noticed that the dates had been post-dated for a month from now. Someone—probably some mob interest in Chicago—had a notary in their hip pocket.

But it was the names listed at the bottom that threw me for a loop. Four of them were unfamiliar, but definitely Italian. However, the two names registered as signatories for the *Knickerbocker Wrestling Federation*—one in particular—caused my jaw to drop.

It told me everything I needed to know about Manny Greenstreet's murder. And it also pointed to the likelihood of another murder that was about to take place—probably before the sun rose in the morning.

Unless I did something about it.

I rolled up the document and tucked it inside my jacket. It was likely that I would have to come back to this office later tonight and return the Merger and Acquisitions Form to the safe, but for now, I had plans for it.

Using Bomberg's telephone, I called for a cab to meet me at a spot near Union Square. I returned the rest of the files to the safe and was about to close the door to the Hercules when a thought occurred to me.

Two more unannounced visits were in my future tonight. Both could prove dangerous—even life-threatening. Seeing how I would have to come back to this office anyway, I might as well borrow some leverage for the time being. Why take chances?

I grabbed the .32 automatic and slipped it into my waistband.

———◦○◦———

34

I GAVE THE CABBIE directions to the general vicinity without giving a specific address. It took only minutes to get there. Once he pulled away, I walked to my target—the first address that I had memorized from the phone book in the Rexall Drugstore earlier in the day.

The neighborhood was upper-middle-class. Brownstones wall-to-wall. I found the house number and studied the place for several minutes. Slumber soaked the block. Not a soul in sight. No lights on inside.

I eased up the stoop to the front door. After inspecting the edges of the doorway for an alarm and finding none, I got out my lock-picks and was inside within a minute, quietly closing the door behind me.

I stood rock still for two full minutes. The lights were out, but there was enough ambient illumination to make out the breakdown of the rooms and the furniture scattered about. A familiar odor permeated the place—a dangerous odor. I recognized it immediately. And I was glad that I'd brought my secret weapon. I unzipped my jacket pocket and allowed my fingers to grab hold of it.

I needed to be ready for any attack that might come.

A staircase off to the right ran up to the second story. A carpet runner covered the steps, which I was glad to see; carpet muffles footfalls, making me nearly soundless.

Slowly, one step at a time, I made my way up the stairs, cautiously placing my weight to keep loose boards from squeaking. I reached the second story and paused to get my bearings. Looking around, I had my choice of four doors.

I was about to choose the nearest one when a noise to my left sent an eerie chill up my spine.

A low gurgling voice breathed from the shadows, a hiss.

Slowly, I turned toward it. A pair of eyes knifed across the landing. Vicious. Angry.

Making no sudden moves, I eased the weapon from my jacket pocket; guarding it with my concealed side. With one hand, I loosened the string that held it. Butcher paper dropped to the floor.

The hiss became a growl. Menacing.

With a measured motion, I skidded the T-bone steak that I had purchased earlier at Heymann's Butcher across the polished floor towards the hissing noise.

The meat swiveled to a stop halfway between us.

A dog eased out from the shadows, sniffing. A springer spaniel, old, waddling, wary, crawled up to the steak and began licking it; his tail wagged. Scooping up the meat in his teeth, he ran off to a corner to have dinner.

Breaking into an unknown residence can be an iffy proposition, and encountering a dog is always a possibility. Dog odor had hit me the moment I came through the front door. A stop at the butcher shop beforehand is a wise precaution. But even then, some dogs can't be bought with such tricks. The mean ones would rather eat your throat than red meat. I lucked out this time.

With the dog occupied, I quickly made a survey of the doors on the second story and soon found the bedroom that I wanted. Through a crack in the doorway, I slipped in as smooth as water flowing through a conduit.

Positioned on the other side of the room was a large poster bed. Two humps laid motionless under the covers. A man and a woman. An obnoxious snore cut through the dark. From where I stood, I couldn't tell which hump was the culprit.

Now here's the thing...if ever I find myself in a residential bedroom that is occupied by sleeping homeowners, I inevitably experience a clash of emotions. As I've mentioned before, my Pops was killed in a situation just like this. His shoes squeaked, and he got plugged for it. Irony aside, you don't have to be a psychiatrist to appreciate the issues that surface in moments like these.

At the top of the list, of course, is remorse, the sorrow of Pops being gone.

But there's also a latent terror that creeps in. Normally I carry out my nighttime visits with confidence and a sense of calm—as if I was built for this kind of life. But this particular scenario—sleeping occupants—causes my blood to race and my mind to hallucinate potential outcomes. Possibly the sleeping man also keeps a snub-nose .38 in his nightstand—just like the guy who had shot Pop. If it could happen to him, it could happen to me. Pops was the best, and I'll forever be in his shadow.

But another emotion floats in my subconscious as well, a tender and pleasant emotion: a sense of intimacy.

As idiotic as it may sound, the replication of the same circumstances that caused Pops' demise somehow draws me closer to him. As if I'm carrying on his legacy. As if he's guiding me, not only with the childhood training he drilled into me, but also by the critical mistakes he made, too.

I can almost hear his voice. His suggestions. His warnings.

The main one being: *don't wear new shoes to a job.*

My crepes didn't make a sound.

At the doorway, I took a moment to collect myself. It wouldn't do to go slobbering over Pops now. I needed to do what I came to do and get out. And fortunately, tonight there was a major difference between now and Pop's circumstances.

I had an Iver Johnson Hammerless Automatic tucked into the waistband of my trousers.

———◆———

35

I SIDLED OVER TO the closet. My primary target.

It was a walk-in with a set of folding doors. Slowly, I eased one open. The top pinion scraped along the metal runner in protest. Within the quiet of the room, it echoed like the hinges of a rusty car door.

Holding my breath, I watched the humps on the bed for movement. No one stirred. The obnoxious snore continued, which was much louder than the scraping noise I'd just made. Even so, I waited a full minute. The last thing I needed was to be surprised while inside the closet.

The opening I had created was just wide enough for my body. I slid in. The closet inside was inky black. Now I had to choose between two poor options: leave the door open and be left somewhat exposed, or re-close it with that annoying screech filling the room.

Reluctantly, I left it ajar.

However, I wasn't about to turn on the closet light; instead, I brought out my penlight. The glare of it filled the space with more than enough illumination. The closet wasn't huge for a walk-in, but it had enough room to move around in. I could tell immediately that three walls were dedicated to the woman of the house and only one to the man—as usual. I headed for that wall.

I was working on a hunch that I could find critical evidence of a crime here, and it would be in the form of blood spatter.

An upper rod held a row of suits, shirts, and slacks. On the floor below was a shoe rack containing about eight pairs of shoes. Squatting down, I ran the penlight over each pair and found exactly what I was looking for: a pair of brown oxfords with a few faint spatters of blood across the toe of one of them. An attempt had been made to wipe some of the blood off, but the shoe hadn't been thoroughly cleaned and polished...yet.

Lifting it from the rack, I turned it over to examine the sole, and sure enough, smeared within the tread, was more blood.

It looked like I'd found our murderer.

I replaced the shoe to the rack, but as I was standing up, a tiny refraction caught my eye. It came from the other shoe next to it. Bending down, I studied the shoe closely without touching it. There, wedged between the laces and the tongue, was a thin fragment of broken glass. The shard was tiny, less than a quarter of an inch long, a sliver really.

Closing my eyes, I pictured the crime scene in my mind. The twisted body. The bashed-in head. The blood and brain matter spattered about. And yes...

Greenstreet's eyeglasses laying off to the side; one lens shattered to pieces.

Was this a fragment from those eyeglasses? Most likely, yes. However, I would leave that up to the police and their forensic unit to decide. My job, for the moment, was to swing the police toward the actual murderer somehow and away from Gus. And any extra evidence to help in that persuasion was an added benefit.

Which included my next task.

A key piece of evidence needed to be here for the police to find—evidence not planted, really, but *returned* to the killer.

I stood to look over the suits hanging on the rod, hoping to find a specific one, one that I was convinced I'd seen before. A cursory glance told me that the suit wasn't here—both the color and pattern were absent.

I flipped through them again.

Nothing.

That wasn't good.

I checked the trousers hanging there, hoping to at least find the pants that went with the suit. But no. They weren't there either.

Frustration set in. Had the killer hidden the suit? Or destroyed it already? The suit was critical to placing the murderer at the scene, and also how I hoped to help nail the sucker.

Oh well. At least I'd found some evidence with the soiled shoes and the shard from the glasses—even if it was meager and somewhat circumstantial.

That's when I spotted the pile of clothing on the wife's side of the closet. The pile seemed out of place with the rest of the room, which was neat and orderly. This was a heap of garments strewn haphazardly across a chair.

Then it came to me. The pile was possibly laundry, set aside to go to the cleaners.

Stepping over to the chair, I swept the penlight over the garments. On top were skirts, dresses, and blouses. But peeking out from underneath were the shirt sleeves of a few dress shirts that belonged to a man. Digging into the heap, I found exactly what I was looking for: a torn suit coat.

The front pocket torn from stem-to-stern. It hung like a flopping tongue. Blood spatters spotted one sleeve.

The suit coat I'd seen before.

———◆◇◆———

36

SEEING THE SUIT COAT confirmed that I had nearly run headlong into the murderer last night.

I had seen him on the street, and I suspect he'd seen me, too.

It had been the drunk that I'd spotted coming down the block just before breaking into the wrestling building. Only, he hadn't been drunk at all; he'd only been unsettled because of the violence he'd just wreaked. The man had limped and staggered, possibly from twisting an ankle, or more likely, from pulling a muscle while swinging a desk leg with all his might. After all, he wasn't fit and brutish like a wrestler; he was softer, like a lawyer.

Bernard Bomberg.

My guess is that Bernie Bomberg hadn't planned on killing Greenstreet last night. It just sort of happened.

Make no mistake, he had always planned on Manny's demise; he simply never intended doing it himself. Why should he? A guy from Chicago was coming to handle that task for him. It was all part of the plot to seize control of the wrestling club's interests.

But somehow things got out of hand in Manny's office. It could be that Manny somehow learned of the plot. Or maybe Bernie couldn't wait. Maybe they argued. Only the two of them know exactly what took place in that office—and Manny ain't talking.

My theory was that Bernie Bomberg panicked.

He might have imagined that Manny had discovered the plot. Manny had just opened the safe in his office. Bernie spotted the handgun inside and possibly thought Manny was reaching for it. So Bernie grabbed the first available weapon, a desk leg, and...BAM. Manny goes down. And at that point, he was committed, so he didn't stop. He kept swinging until the deed was done.

He then grabbed everything from the safe, including the pistol, and ran it up to his office, where he locked everything up, along with his contract deal with the people from Chicago and the down payment they had given him. Panicked and in a hurry, he had left the light on when leaving his office. He just wanted to get out of there.

Minutes later, I had spotted him stumbling away from the crime scene.

But the torn pocket of his suit jacket had stuck out to me. It must have happened during the scuffle in the office. Possibly, Greenstreet had snagged the garment as he fell to the floor. His hand got hooked, and the pocket tore open.

And something tumbled out.

I reached into my A1 aviator jacket to retrieve the item.

The train ticket stub, for the 10:45 arrival of the 20th Century Limited, that I'd found under the body. It must have hit the floor before Greenstreet did and got wedged under him. Bomberg never realized it.

Bernie Bomberg did *not* arrive on the train this morning, as he had told the police. He'd caught an earlier train and had arrived last night.

Just in time to kill his brother-in-law.

But he had an alibi, right? He had shown Crenshaw proof.

No. I knew he didn't have an alibi at all.

Bomberg, of course, had been one of the two men that I had overheard talking in the abandoned building this morning. He had been the one with the softer voice. And he had told the man with the gravelly voice that he hadn't been home yet, hadn't slept. Why? Because he had wandered the streets all night. He couldn't go home. His wife would know he'd taken an earlier train.

While eavesdropping on the conversation, I had heard Bomberg ask a strange question of Gravelly-voice: 'Do you have the ticket that I asked you to bring?'

The other man had told him it was no good anymore, but Bomberg disagreed. He needed it.

My guess is that Mr. Gravelly-voice had just arrived on the morning train from Chicago, and Bomberg was asking for his ticket stub. He needed it as proof that he'd only come into town that morning. It was his 'Get-out-of-jail-free' card.

Not quite.

Opening up the torn jacket, I tucked the ticket for last night's 20th Century Limited 10:45 arrival into the inside breast pocket. I then replaced the rest of the clothing on top of the suit. Hopefully, before the night is out, I could somehow arrange for the police to find it. And it had to happen before Mrs. Bomberg made a trip to the cleaners.

I clicked off my penlight.

I'd found everything I'd come to find, and returned everything I'd meant to return. It was time to leave. But as I turned to exit the closet, I halted in mid-step.

A shadow was moving across the carpet outside the open closet door.

37

MY ADRENALIN SPIKED. My throat went dry.

Someone was out there. I could see movement, that's for sure. But had they already spotted me?

Fear paralyzed me. It was Pops all over again. Someone must have awoken and caught the glow of the penlight shining through the opening of the closet.

I remained deathly still for two minutes, watching the shadow play across the carpet outside, waiting for the closet door to explode open.

But it didn't, and I grew curious.

The shadow had become stationary and yet seemed to flutter at the same time. As if whoever stood out there had a nervous tic they couldn't control. Maybe they had already called the police and had a handgun that they weren't used to holding. They were scared. It made them shake. Even so, it appeared they intended to outlast me. Or shoot me as I came out.

I wasn't about to let that happen.

My hand went for the grip of the automatic. I eased it from my waistband.

Edging up to the opening, I lifted the pistol up and cautiously peeked around the corner of the door frame—fully expecting to encounter violence.

But none came.

Instead, I found a Springer Spaniel. He sat there with his head cocked and his tail wagging—the fluttering shadow waffling across the carpet. In his mouth were the remains of the steak I'd brought for him—just the bone.

He eyed me as if I were his new best friend. But when I went to give him a pet, his eyes narrowed, and he snarled around the bone. I put my hands up in mock surrender, and he turned to scamper off.

Snoring continued to fill the room.

It didn't look like I was going to get plugged tonight, at least not in this house. But I wasn't so sure about my next stop.

Of my three scheduled break-ins, the next would be the most dangerous.

Fortunately, I still had the Iver Johnson Automatic. I tucked it back into my waistband and quietly left the Bomberg residence.

38

———◦○◦———

I watched the apartment building from across the street. Through the glass doors, I could see the lobby. It was quiet inside. However, I knew I couldn't enter through the lobby. I had learned from my earlier conversation with Crenshaw that a doorman lurked inside—an observant doorman—and I would never get past him. Plus, I didn't want an encounter with him and leave behind a potential witness.

Instead, I strolled down the block to an adjacent building, let myself in, and went up to the roof. I clambered over to the next rooftop and found a ladder that ran down the side of the building to a fire-escape. Climbing down the fire-escape, I came to the floor I wanted and entered through a hallway window.

Recalling the apartment number I had memorized earlier, I found the door, retrieved my lock-picks, and let myself in.

No dog this time. But I didn't expect one. The person living here wasn't the type to keep pets.

I wended my way through the apartment until I found the bedroom door. It was already ajar, and I could hear sleep noises coming from inside the room. I slipped in and surveyed the place.

My hand hovered near the grip of the automatic. Ready for anything.

The bed was placed against the far wall. There were two humps under the covers.

Sleeping occupants again.

Only this time, the specter of Pops getting shot wouldn't be haunting me. I wanted to be discovered. I wasn't here to sneak around the apartment so much as to have a conversation.

The bedroom had a window. For a thief, depending on the circumstances, windows can be an asset or a liability. It's a liability if people on the outside can witness activities taking place on the inside. However, it can be an asset if you need entry or a means of escape. This window was open. Lacy curtains billowed gently in the evening breeze. I stepped over to it and peered through. Outside, just below the window sill, a narrow ledge ran along the face of the building.

This window had just become an asset, in case I needed to beat a fast retreat.

In the corner, to my left, was a dresser, and next to it was a wooden chair with articles of clothing strewn across it. I walked over, tipped the chair slightly, dumping the clothes onto the floor.

I carried the chair over to the bed and quietly set it next to the larger of the two sleeping humps, placing it with the back towards the bed—a little extra barrier between me and the larger hump. I straddled the chair with my arms draped over the back.

I withdrew the hammerless automatic and licked my lips.

This was where things could go south.

———◆———

39

REACHING OVER, I NUDGED the man snoring there.

He squirmed a bit, batting a slumber-soaked hand toward the nudge as if addressing an unwelcome pest. He continued to snore.

I nudged him again, but this time I said aloud, "Wake up stupid."

He gurgled and twisted a semiconscious look my way. His eyes blinked twice before his mind bridged from sleep to awareness to complete alertness. A pretty short bridge.

He lurched up, his eyes bulging with terror as he grasped the reality of a pistol being pointed at his midsection. He was shirtless, his upper torso thick with muscles that were now flexed in trepidation.

"What the hell?" he croaked, his voice crusted with sleep.

"Don't move, Mickey," I whispered, speaking with more calm than I felt. "This thing goes off pretty easy," I added—just like a tough guy would.

"Who are you and how did you get...? Wait...you're that guy from the diner today," he said.

"Yep, that's me."

"The one that was following me," he added weakly.

I remained quiet. I recalled Nick's warning about the man: *Stay away from him...I was told...he has a temper like gasoline*. But suddenly, it seemed like I didn't have to worry about it so much. As big as he was, and with a gun pointed at him, he looked more like soda pop than gasoline. He was scared spit-less.

"Look," he stammered, "It doesn't have to go down this way."

"Oh?" I asked. "Go down what way?" The guy looked petrified.

"Chicago can have my side of the business if that's what you want. I'll sign it over right now. Just don't kill me. Not like this."

"Shut up," I said. "We have some things to discuss."

"What things?"

The hump on the other side of him stirred. A woman lifted her head to peer over at me. Suddenly she was wide awake, too. She lurched up just like Jacobs had; she was shirtless too. Her breasts bounced with the same trepidation that Mickey's muscles had. I liked her show better.

"What's going on, Mickey?" she whimpered.

It was the same girl from Woolworth's, *Florence Fighting-gale*, yet without the nurse's uniform, or any uniform of any kind. She made some impression sitting up like that, her sleep-tousled hair curling around her pretty face, and her striking blue eyes wide with concern. Some of her make-up had rubbed off and her black eye was shining through. She made no move to cover herself.

"Shut up, Flo," muttered Mickey. He trained his eyes on the automatic.

"Wait," she yelped as she looked me over, recognizing me. "It's you. What are you doing here now?"

Her question was almost the expected response to being awakened in the middle of the night by a guy with a pistol. Normal. Except for the very end. That last word got my attention. *Now?* Not, 'What are you doing here?' But, 'What are you doing here *now*?'

That tiny word told me everything I needed to know. I grinned at the realization.

"Why would I be here...now?" I asked.

"Because," she croaked. "It's..."

"Because it's not supposed to happen like this?"

Her lips tightened. A flicker of fear flit across her face. As if plans were violently veering off course.

"I think what we have here is a case of mistaken identity," I said. "You think I'm somebody I'm not."

Mickey Jacobs gave me a curious squint. She did too.

And in a flash, yes, things went south.

Funny how you can have full control of a situation one moment, and the next you do not.

My mistake had primarily been one of focus. My attention—my eye, my gun—was aimed at the larger of the two naked people. I had forgotten altogether that the smaller, female person was, in fact, a professional athlete, and trained in a sport that can administer violence in a split second.

And that was all it took. A split second. The two of them tag-teamed me.

Nimble wrestler that she was, Nurse Flo snapped up on one arm, her exquisite breasts bouncing, as her leg—her scrumptious naked leg—kicked out from beneath the sheet, round-housed my way, clearing Mickey completely, and smashed the pistol clear out of my hand.

Dumbfounded, I blinked toward the automatic skittering across the floor.

Turning back, the last thing I witnessed was Mickey Jacob's fist slamming into my face.

Tag-teamed.

40

I WAS ONLY OUT for a few seconds, but long enough for the room dynamics to change entirely.

They had knocked me clear of the chair; I laid on the floor, crumpled up against the wall by the nightstand. Jacobs loomed above me, his arms spread in a fighter stance. His fists white-knuckle hot. He was still shirtless, but he'd found a pair of trousers somewhere.

Flo was nowhere to be seen.

"Where's Flo?" I asked. My left eye socket thudded with pain. I winced.

"In the other room, calling the police," he sneered.

"Oh, I can guarantee she's not doing that."

"What do you mean by that?" he spat.

"The last thing she wants is the police here."

He stared, dumbfounded.

"When did you two get married, Mickey?"

For a brief second, his rigid posture slumped like a question mark, but quickly snapped back.

"W...what? How did you know we got married? Nobody knows about that."

"Ah...but I know. So does Bomberg."

"Bernie...our lawyer? How?"

"We need to talk about your wife, Mickey," I said. I moved to get up.

"Stay where you are," he seethed. His right fist cocked back. He seemed to grow larger as his anger swelled. "I'll put you down again."

"Probably," I said. "My eye hurts like hell. I'm going to have a shiner tomorrow. Did you give Flo the shiner she has?"

He looked stunned. "Me? I wouldn't hit a woman. She got that in the ring the other night."

"She's selling you out, Mickey." I looked around the floor for the automatic, but it was gone. The only thing near me was a pillow that had fallen off the bed. Pillows don't make for much of a weapon.

"What the hell are you talking about?"

"Can I show you something?"

He didn't respond, just glowered.

"I'm going to reach into my pocket—real slow like—to hand you some reading material. You know how to read, don't you, Mickey?"

He still didn't respond, which I took to be a go-ahead.

I eased my hand into my jacket. His fist cocked back further. Slowly, I brought out the contract that I'd taken from Bomberg's office safe. Instead of handing it to him, I set it on the edge of the bed, like a peace offering.

As I retreated back to the floor, I moved my right hand over to the pillow, grabbing it by the corner.

"It's a merger and acquisitions form for the purchase of your wrestling outfit. Go ahead, look at how it's signed at the bottom of the last page."

He took up the document and unfolded it. He kept one fist curled. He scanned the pages, stopping on the last. He blinked.

"Notice the signature right next to Bernard Bomberg. It says, Florence Jacobs—your new wife. Both signatories are listed as the major stakeholders in the Knickerbocker Wrestling Federation. Also, notice that they postdated the form for a month from now. It won't be legal until after the funeral."

He shot an alarmed glance at me. "What funeral?"

"Yours, of course. You think she's in the next room calling the police? She's not. She's calling Bomberg."

"Bernie? Why would she do that?"

"To warn him."

"About what?"

"That I've messed up their plans for getting rid of you."

His mouth opened like a fish. Nothing came out.

"As you can see, she and Bernie are selling the Knickerbocker outfit to the Italians."

"They can't do that. They have no say in it."

"Ah, but they do Mickey...at least, they will, once you're out of the picture. You see, Manny's stake in the club is going to his sister, Velma—that's Bernie's wife. But I can guarantee that Bernie controls her strings. I'm sure he has a tidy little 'power of attorney' document in his files to take care of that end. But then there's your stake. They've worked it so that once you're gone, your half goes to your wife. Bernie has been in talks with the people in Chicago, but now it's way beyond the talk stage. They're paying big money. Look at the contract, you lunkhead. It's already done. Bernie received forty thousand dollars cash as a down payment. It's in his safe right now. I saw it with my own two eyes."

I watched his Adam's apple bob. His eyes went to the contract again.

"But neither Manny nor I wanted to sell the Italians," he said weakly. "We were merging with Big Bob."

"That's what Manny wanted?" I asked.

He nodded. "Yeah, it was all set. They set us both up to get management roles in Big Bob's outfit. That way, we'd get a good amount of front money, but still be in the business."

Nick had been wrong. Sort of. Nick's lawyer had told him that Manny was looking for other options because that's what he had heard from Bomberg, who actually *was* exploring other options. But he was doing it behind Greenstreet and Jacob's backs. Manny and Mickey had been on the same page all along.

"Big Bob Barton warned us at lunch about a double-cross," I said. "And there it is."

He squinted at me. "Who are you?"

"I'm just a guy who got caught in the middle. I'm friends with *The Storming Swede*."

"Who's that?"

"The prizefighter that Manny tried to swindle into becoming a wrestler."

"Oh...that guy. The one who tore the place up."

"The police think the Swede killed Manny. But he didn't. Bernie killed him—just like he plans to kill you. But this time he won't be getting his hands dirty. It's a contract job. The Italians are doing him a favor. A few minutes ago, your wife mistook me for a hitman from Chicago—just like Big Bob Barton had yesterday afternoon. In the diner, I thought Flo was flirting with me at Woolworths, but she wasn't. She thought I was the guy, and she was pointing you out to me."

Jacobs's face went into calculation mode. I could see him adding it up.

"Did you hear the question she asked a few minutes ago when she first spotted me? She said, 'What are you doing here *now*?' You see, *now* wasn't the planned time for the hit. My guess is that it's supposed to happen just before the 20th Century Limited leaves for Chicago tomorrow morning. That's when the hitman is leaving town. Before nine o'clock."

He continued to stare at me. Digesting the information.

"I think he's planning to take both you and Big Bob out at the same time. That's why Big Bob has his two guys with him at all times. He's just as worried about getting whacked as you should be. When is the next time you are to meet with Big Bob, by the way?"

"Tomorrow morning at six o'clock, at a diner a few blocks from here."

"Is Flo going?"

"No, she's..." His face slacked.

"There you go. It would've happened yesterday at Woolworth's, except Flo was at the table. Which was fortunate for you."

"But why would she do this?"

"Because I don't want to wrestle no more, Mickey," came a sultry voice from across the room.

We both swung a look that way.

In the bedroom doorway, her curvaceous silhouette was back-lit by the lights blazing from the other room. She now wore a wispy silk robe, transparent in the backlight, showcasing her naked form underneath. Beautiful. Simply beautiful. A lethal beautiful.

From the floor I sneered, "Aw gee, Mickey, why did you give her the gun?"

———————◦———————

41

"WHAT'S GOING ON, BABY?" asked Jacobs.

He took a step toward her. The automatic swiveled to meet him.

"Stay put, Mickey," she said. "Don't make me shoot you."

"Aw baby, you wouldn't do that."

"Wouldn't I? This thing is going down, one way or another."

"What thing? Is this true?" He waved the contract at her.

"You wouldn't listen to me, Mickey. How many times did I tell you I didn't want to wrestle no more? How many times?" she screeched.

Jacobs stayed quiet.

My eyes remained drilled on the automatic. The way I figured it, while we sat around and chatted, a hitman from Chicago—Mr. Gravelly Voice—was on his way to this apartment. He could be here any minute now.

"I was sick of it," wailed Flo. "Wrestling is worse than stripping for a living."

"What are you talking about?" asked Jacobs. "I got you out of that business. I told you, burlesque was no kind of life for you. Not for my wife."

"No kind of life? Ha. At least when I was taking off my clothes, I wasn't getting hurt all the time. I've broken my nose, my ribs, and two fingers. Look at my eye, Mickey! Look at it! You wouldn't let me stop. Then when we had the chance to sell out...you wouldn't do it. I begged you. But no, you wanted to hand me over to Big Bob instead." She shuddered. "And you know what else he's after—the fat creep."

"He was going to make you a star, baby."

"I didn't want to be a star!" she screamed. "I kept telling you that."

"So you thought the answer was to have me killed?"

"I thought the answer was to take the money and run. I begged you to take it so we could run together. But you wouldn't. I wanted out, one way or another."

"But...to knock me off?"

"It's just business, Mickey. Just business."

I could've listened to the melodrama all night. It was better than the radio show *Cavalcade of America*. But we didn't have time for soap operas.

In one snap, I let fly the pillow toward the doorway. I was on my feet in a flash.

But not before the pistol fired. And it fired twice.

———◆———

42

THE CRACKS OF BOTH shots blistered into the room like thunder.

Both bullets struck targets.

The first got Mickey Jacobs. The second got the pillow.

Blood spattered.

Feathers flew.

I had just cleared the foot of the bed when I caught a blur of motion to my left. Mickey, wounded and bleeding but still on his feet, lunged at his wife. His fist slammed into her face. The gun fired as his fist connected. But I couldn't tell if that bullet struck a target or not. But I certainly heard the girl's face getting crunched.

Flo crumpled to the floor as if boneless.

I froze in mid-step.

The room smelled of gunpowder. It snowed feathers. Four seconds of destruction.

Mickey loomed above Flo like a boxer over a defeated opponent. His chest heaving. His left shoulder seeping blood. He appeared not to notice it.

Flo groaned. Her face twitched and her hands flopped some, but her eyes remained shut. She was out.

"I thought you didn't hit women?" I said.

"Only dames who try taking me out," he answered bitterly.

"Are you okay?" I asked, looking at his wound. "Did that third shot get you?"

"No," he said simply.

He reached down and picked up the automatic. He squinted at it.

"We have a gun just like this," he said.

"Yeah, that's the one you own. Bomberg took it from the office safe last night. And I took it from his safe tonight."

"So Bernie really killed Manny?"

I nodded.

"Bastard." He looked at his wife and shook his head. "She was going to kill me."

I stepped up to him, cautious-like.

"Look," I said. "We don't have much time. Someone in the building probably heard those shots. And Flo called Bomberg. I'm sure of it. That means Bomberg likely called his guy from Chicago to come clean things up. He'll be coming through your front door to take you out. I overheard him talking with Bomberg this morning. He's the one that followed you to Woolworth's. I just followed him there and got caught up in things."

Jacobs slanted me a look and then looked back at the gun in his hand.

"I don't care how you handle things from here," I said, "but keep me out of it. The cops are going to be here eventually, and you're going to have to adjust your story concerning Bomberg. You need to get the cops to issue a search warrant for his house and office as soon as possible—it has to happen before morning."

"How can I do that?"

"That's up to you. Make something up, tell them Flo let it slip about Bomberg, anything, but get the cops over to Bomberg's place! All kinds of evidence can be found in Bomberg's closet. Everything they need to put him at the scene and blow up his alibi."

"How do you know that?"

I grinned. "Just get the cops to his house and to his office. The rest will pan out, believe me."

He looked reluctant. "I'll do what I can."

"Better do more than that, Mickey. They might think that you and Flo were in on it together. You don't want the chair, do you?"

His face curled into concern.

"I need to go," I said. "I can't get caught here. I'm already in hot water with the investigating detective."

"Yeah, I saw him arrest you yesterday."

"He was just throwing his weight around. But I can't afford to run into him again."

"Okay. But Flo might talk."

"She probably will, but she'll have other problems to deal with. Accessory to murder for one and attempted murder for another."

I reached down to the floor and picked up the Merger and Acquisition Forms. Fortunately, the contract had avoided blood spatter. I folded it up and tucked it into my jacket.

"Hey, where you going with that?" he yelped.

"I have to return it to Bernie's safe tonight. Believe me, you want the police to find it there and not here. It's evidence that will help send Bernie to the chair. I would take the gun with me too, but seeing how it was just used to shoot you, it would be harder to explain how it got back in the safe than how it got here. You'll have to make something up about that too. Tell the cops you were mistaken about it being in the safe...that you had it all along. Or tell them Bernie took it and gave it to Flo. It'll be her word against yours. I don't care. Just don't tell them you got it from me."

He nodded solemnly. "How can I get in contact with you?"

"You can't. I'm nameless. As far as you're concerned, I was mere smoke passing through. Oh. By the way, I want you to tell the cops something very specific."

"What?"

I leaned in and whispered my instructions.

He blinked. "Okay."

"Don't forget."

"I won't."

Stepping over Flo, still passed out on the floor, I started towards the bedroom door to leave through the living room, but stopped cold.

A faint scraping noise came from the other room. I recognized it immediately. Someone was playing with the front door lock.

I turned to Jacobs. "The hit-man is here already."

He grit his teeth. His glare hardened. The automatic came up.

"I got this," he muttered as he brushed past me.

He charged through the bedroom doorway into the other room.

I couldn't wait around for the show. I had already outstayed my welcome. I turned and headed for the open window—my escape asset.

I was climbing between the billowing curtains when gunshots blasted from the other room. Flashes sparked through the doorway.

But I didn't wait around to learn the score.

I was gone.

43

———◆———

I AWOKE THE NEXT day to pounding—pounding noise and pounding pain. I lifted my head from my pillow, wincing. My head thundered. As I blinked my eyes open, agony radiated across the bone structure of my face. One of my eyes had swollen shut. Repercussions of Mickey Jacobs' right cross. Reaching up to touch it, I recoiled. It was beyond tender.

I could only imagine what Flo's face was like today.

I swung my legs around to the floor. The pounding did not abate. I then realized that the hammering was taking place outside my noggin. The apartment was rattling. Someone was knocking on my door.

I got up, put on my robe, and trudged toward the offending clamor. I opened the door to find Detective Wilbur Crenshaw standing there in all his gnomish glory.

"You look like crap, Bucky," he offered as an opening salvo.

"Good morning to you too, Detective," I said.

"Morning? It's two-thirty in the afternoon."

"Is it?"

He stepped around me and into my apartment as if invited. "What happened to your eye? Someone slug ya?"

"I got mugged," I muttered.

He snorted at that. "First the Swede, then you. Everyone's getting mugged these days."

"And I still have yet to see a single mugger being arrested, Wilbur."

Suddenly my throat felt constricted, parched. I pushed past him to tread zombie-like to the kitchen sink. Turning on the tap, I filled a glass of water and guzzled. The cat appeared at the window, hunching its back and rubbing up against the glass.

"You disobeyed me yesterday," said Crenshaw off-handedly.

"In what way?"

He was standing at the kitchen table behind me. On top of the table was Gus's suitcase, still open from yesterday. Much of his stuff remained strewn about. Crenshaw, as if returning to finish a forgotten chore, began replacing the articles back into the case—a job he'd begun before receiving his revelation of Gus's whereabouts yesterday afternoon.

"You didn't stay put as I told you to," he said, pushing the pair of boxing gloves into the case. "You left the apartment."

I drank another glass of water to keep my mouth from answering him. I could feel his eyes on me. Once I had drained the water, I set down the glass and opened the window to let the cat in.

"I came back to pick you up. But you weren't here. Where did you go, Bucky?"

"I don't remember."

"What do you mean, you don't remember?"

"Look, you didn't arrest me, did you? No! So I thought of it more as a request than a command. I needed some fresh air. So I went out and got mugged."

The cat jumped up on the table, sniffing into the case and the items in it. Crenshaw brushed him aside, but the cat wasn't having it. He climbed into the case on top of Gus's yellow robe and laid down.

Giving up on the re-packing job, Crenshaw turned to lean against the table with his arms folded. "We had some developments last night," he said.

I didn't look at him. I stared out the window at the fire-escape.

"We arrested the person who killed Manny Greenstreet."

I remained quiet.

"You don't seem very interested," he said snidely.

I turned to him. "I just woke up, Wilbur. Let me guess, it wasn't Gus."

"No. It was Greenstreet's lawyer, Bernard Bomberg, that did it. He's confessed and everything."

"Oh?"

"Yeah. He broke down once we got into his house with a search warrant and found some evidence. It seems his alibi wasn't so good after all. He came in on an earlier train. He tried tricking us with another ticket stub. It seems he was trying to steal the wrestling outfit out from under Manny Greenstreet and Mickey Jacobs, so he could sell it to some corporate interests in Chicago. That nurse wrestler, *Florence Fighting-gale* was in on it with him."

"Sounds like quite a plot."

He eyed me coolly. "There was a shootout at Mickey Jacob's apartment last night—well...really, this morning, around three-thirty."

I ordered my face to remain still. With the throbbing in my eye socket, I couldn't tell if it was working.

"Jacobs killed a guy named Antonio Moretti. It was self-defense. The other guy had a gun. We suspect that Moretti's connected to the Italian mob, and that they sent here him to kill Jacobs, and possibly Big Bob Barton. But Mickey got the drop on him. Seems that the .32 automatic hadn't been stolen from the safe after all. His girlfriend had it. She shot Jacobs with it just before Moretti showed up. Tried to kill Jacobs herself. Can you believe that?"

"Where's Gus?" I asked.

Ignoring me, he said, "We found a contract for the sale of the wrestling club in the lawyer's safe. A boatload of cash, too. We're checking on the corporate interest listed in the paperwork. It appears to be a shell corporation attached to the Italian mob."

"Where's Gus?" I repeated.

"He's still downtown. We're letting him go. Nick Terrano is with him now. We'll bring him around later. I wanted to chat with you first."

"About what?"

Wilbur pulled out a chair and took a seat. "I'm still trying to figure out what role you played in all this."

"How many times do I have to tell you, Wilbur? I played the role of Good Samaritan. I gave a guy a bologna sandwich—then you arrested him for murder."

Crenshaw shook a finger at me. "No. No. No. Your fingerprints are all over this thing."

"You found my prints? Where?" Panic gripped me. Had I forgotten something?

"Not your actual prints, idiot. I'm speaking metaphorically."

"Oh." I relaxed some.

"For example, Nurse Flo started yammering about an intruder breaking into their apartment last night."

"Was it the same intruder Mickey Jacobs shot? The Italian guy?"

"No." He studied me. "Another fellow. She claims it was the same guy that Big Bob Barton slapped around at Woolworth's yesterday."

I tried to look shocked, but again the eye socket pain impeded the overall effect. "She tried dragging me into it? Why would she do that?"

Crenshaw shrugged. "I don't know. But she was adamant about it. Said it was you. Jacobs refused to corroborate her story. He told us she made it up. To try to claim someone else shot him, and not her."

"Ah. She wanted to put the blame on me. But she shot Mickey...right?"

"Oh, she pulled the trigger, okay. We found gun residue."

"Well, there you go," I said. "I hate it when people lie, don't you?" I turned to fill my glass with tap water again.

"There was one more thing," he said.

I began sipping water and staring at the fire escape again.

"Mickey Jacobs suddenly remembered all sorts of details that he hadn't mentioned yesterday when I had questioned him for three hours. He's the one that led us to Bomberg. Told us it was urgent to check the lawyer's house and office."

I shrugged. "So?"

"He told us one thing that I found very odd."

"What's that? Don't wear a Taylor on your face?"

He let out a hiss. "No. He specifically told us that sometimes Bomberg closes his safe without twisting the dial to lock it, and that we should just try opening it first before calling in a locksmith. And wouldn't you know it? His safe was already unlocked. The door just swung open."

I turned to look him in the eye. "That's pretty stupid. A guy could get robbed that way."

He held my gaze. "That's right. Someone could've robbed Bomberg blind. There was forty-eight thousand dollars in that safe. Quite a temptation. Just think...if a thief happened by, he could've just opened the door and taken it all. And odds are, we would have never found the culprit who did it."

"Good thing nobody got there before you," I offered.

Crenshaw stood. Hitched up his belt. Tapped the brim of his hat back on his forehead. And smiled, yes, actually smiled at me.

"Have a good day, Bucky."

———◆———

44

THE NEXT MORNING, THICK clouds loomed over the skyscrapers like approaching tanks. No rain, just dreary gray clouds.

Gus and I headed to Whitey's for breakfast. Gus had slept on my couch again. He'd tried giving me that 'I don't take charity' line again, but I informed him we were now friends and friends help each other out. 'Don't rob me of that', I had said. 'You'd be stealing my opportunity to be charitable' (a strange mix of words coming from a thief).

He acquiesced.

Truthfully, I could tell it relieved him. Having spent the night in a jail cell must have softened his principles some, because he barely argued about it. Anything was better than being in the hoosegow.

Besides, Gus didn't know it yet, but his fortunes were about to change.

As we came through the door of Whitey's diner, Billie Holiday greeted us, singing *Summertime* from the white Bakelite radio on the shelf, reminding us that somewhere:

> the living was easy, the fish are jumping, and the cotton is high.

But even Billie's sultry voice wasn't breaking up the clouds over New York.

The crowd in the diner appeared equally dispersed today, making it hard to tell which tables were being serviced by the new waitress—whose section

I was eager to explore. I looked around but didn't see her delightful form anywhere. I didn't see Trudy's not-so-delightful form either.

I shrugged, and we grabbed an empty booth overlooking the street.

As we settled in, Whitey came whipping by with an armload of platters steaming with hot food. He wore an apron over his slacks, white shirt, and bowtie today. The apron left me puzzled.

"Buck, you look horrible," he said in passing.

"You're not so pretty yourself," I offered.

He chuckled at that.

My black-eye had grown to take over one side of my face. The bruise had mottled purple and green, and streaked with veins of broken blood vessels. Gus's bruises had pretty much healed. He looked hale in comparison.

And after depositing the order of platters a few booths down, Whitey came back to our table, withdrawing an order pad from his apron as he drew up to us. "What can I get you, boys?"

"You can get me that new waitress," I said. "That's the only reason I came in."

"Rosy? She's not here yet," he muttered grimly. "She tends to be late every day."

"Oh? Are you going to fire her for it?"

"Heavens, no! The woman's a boon to business. As soon as she clocks in the place fills up."

"Where's Trudy?"

He frowned. "I gave her the week off—with pay. She nearly got into a fistfight with Rosy yesterday afternoon. They don't like each other much."

"Out with the old, in with new," I chuckled.

Whitey grimaced. "I don't think so. Trudy's a far better waitress than Rosy is. I would hate to lose her."

He took our orders, and after he left, I said to Gus, "By the way, you're buying me breakfast today, big guy."

His face went red with embarrassment. "Buck...I'm sorry, but you know as well as anyone that I don't have a plum nickel."

I opened my wallet and handed him two hundred and sixty dollars.

"What's this?" he asked, astonished.

"It's the dough Manny Greenstreet took from you. All of it."

"But...how?"

"Let's just say all the partners involved in the Knickerbocker Wrestling Federation wanted it returned to you in good faith."

"That was very nice of them."

I grinned at his ignorance.

"I also have another gift."

From my jacket pocket, I pulled out both contracts—the one from his suitcase and the one from Bomberg's safe. I slid them across the table.

"You, my friend, are no longer in the wrestling business."

He swept up the contracts and a glow of joy came over him. "But...how?"

"Best you don't ask."

He blinked and opened his mouth as if to protest, but then thought better of it.

"Then it's over?"

"It's over," I said. "You're a free man. You can go back to Minnesota today if you like."

He hesitated. "Yeah...I suppose."

"That's what you wanted, isn't it?"

He shrugged. "I don't know. Two days ago, I was pretty eager to get back home—especially after being arrested. But before that happened, when I was with Nick the other night, we got to talking and...well, I like him."

"Nick's the best," I said.

"Well, now that I don't have to wrestle, I'm thinking I might hang around for a while. Nick told me he would help with my training and maybe set up some bouts for me. Big time bouts. He said I could sleep at the gym until I get my own place. Or..." Gus hesitated. "Or...he said I could stay at his house. But I don't think..."

He trailed off and I could almost see the specters of Francesca and Regina haunting that idea.

Behind me, the bell over the front door tinkled and suddenly I felt, more than saw, the immensity of a presence enter the diner. Gus's eyes widened as he glanced over my shoulder.

"That's one big man," he whispered.

Turning around, I found Big Bob Barton filling the aisle.

"Oh boy," I uttered warily.

His monstrous bullet-shaped head turned on its axis, the half-lidded eyes scoping out the place, as if zeroing in on a specific target. There was no sign of his two hoodlums lurking about. He was flying solo.

When his eyes landed on me, his placid, fat face flickered with recognition. He lumbered our way. When he got to our booth, he trilled his fingers toward Gus as a command to shove over. And like one of his minions, Gus obeyed. Barton plopped himself down and Whitey's Place tilted some. Together on one bench, the two of them looked pretty squished.

He threw a questioning look at my beautifully marred mug.

"Did I do that?" he asked.

"Naw," I said. "Yours was a love tap. This is how Mickey Jacobs says hello."

He grunted. "Yeah, I wanted to talk to you about that." He reached into his side pocket with his fat hands and withdrew something shiny. I caught a flash of metal, and at first, thought it was a small pistol.

He dropped a pair of pliers on the table and pushed them over to me.

"I wanted to return these," he muttered in that low creepy voice of his.

"How did you find me? You didn't even know my name."

"I have ways," he said. And left it at that. "Mickey told me what you did for us."

I shrugged. "I didn't do it for you. I was helping out a friend. You merely reaped the collateral benefits."

"Even so, we didn't treat you too good, and according to Mickey, the two of us might be meat on a slab this morning if it weren't for you. That wop was gunning for us."

"It worked out."

He reached into his jacket again, another movement that made me tense up, but this time he only withdrew an envelope.

"I want to show my appreciation...and apologies." He slid the envelope across the table to me.

I stared at it, but didn't reach for it.

"Go ahead, you earned it."

I picked it up, flipped open the flap, and let loose a low whistle.

I set the envelope down and slid it back across the table.

"I didn't do it for money."

One of his palms came up, and I recoiled because of it, my cheek recalling the slap he'd given me yesterday. It seemed his every movement put me on edge.

"I know, I know, you weren't working for me," he said. "I just wanted to say thank-you. Mickey's wrestling business is staying here in New York. We all will make money. And it's because of you." He tapped the envelope with two fat fingers. "You will take it, or I'll be offended."

"I don't take payment with strings attached," I said. "Cause, no matter what, I still don't work for you."

He shook his big bullet head. "No strings. I get up from here and we don't see each other no more."

I liked that aspect of it.

He pushed the envelope back.

I gave him a nod.

He slid a glance Gus's way. His head tilted, appraising.

"You're a big guy," he said. "Good looking too. You ever think about taking up professional wrestling? I could make you a star."

Boy, if looks could kill, Boulder Bart's bullet head would've exploded into wet confetti.

He got the message.

Big Bob squeezed out of the booth and lumbered off. The aroma in the diner turned pleasant without him. I stuffed the envelope into my jacket pocket. Honest gains for a change...sort of.

Across the table, Gus was giving me a goofy mid-western victory grin. "Looks like you came out ahead too."

"It just about covers the cost of the bologna you ate."

A pink uniform, with a clean white apron, appeared at our table. In front of us, cups and saucers were placed. Black coffee poured into cups.

"Good morning, boys," came a honey-soaked voice.

We both looked up.

Rosy Grace. The new waitress.

She smiled and sunlight sliced through the gray clouds like a prism.

Also by Jonathan Call

 ***Up in Smoke*** – a noir heist mystery

 ***Smoke Get's in My Eyes*** – a noir murder mystery

 ***Where There's Smoke*** – a noir thriller mystery

 ***Smoke 'em Out*** – a noir espionage mystery

Stealing Tesla

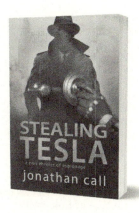

**CRACKING THE WRONG SAFE WAS HIS FIRST MIS-
TAKE...** A cat burglar stumbles across Nikola Tesla's safe,
and the secrets inside hurl him headlong into the world of
espionage and murder.

Enemy agents are willing to kill for those secrets. And the
fate of World War 2 is now in the hands of a thief.

Stealing Tesla – a noir thriller of espionage

Jonathan Call

Jonathan Call is the author of noir thrillers and mysteries. He is also a fine artist, illustrator, and ever-improving musician. He lives with his wife in North Carolina.

"I love the noir world of black and white heroes, antiheroes, and strong-willed femme fatales. At the drop of a hat (make that a fedora) I'll stop to read a pulp mystery or watch a hard-boiled flick from the '40s. Ah...a simpler time of trench-coats, snub nose .38s, and mysteries lurking in the shadows."